Also by Dayne Edmondson

The Dark Tide Trilogy
Emergence
Eclipse
Ruin

The Mageborn Saga
Mageborn
The Cursed Tower
Halls of Light

The Seven Stars Universe
Ghost Ranger
Space Commando

The Shadow Trilogy
Blood and Shadows
Time of Shadows
Shadows Fall

Standalone
The Complete Dark Tide Trilogy
The Complete Shadow Trilogy

Watch for more at https://www.darkstarpublishing.com.

Table of Contents

Ruin

Written by: Dayne Edmondson

Published by Dark Star Publishing
Edited by Jennifer Ingman
Cover design by Matt Forsyth

Join our mailing list

J oin our mailing list by visiting http://eepurl.com/b7th21 and signing up. You will receive a free copy of the first issue of SciFan Magazine for FREE. SciFan Magazine is packed with science fantasy stories from very talented authors.

Chapter 1 - Fire and Light

A ball of reddish-yellow flame slammed into an invisible wall, curving around it. The flames flew outward and extinguished, leaving only the afterglow imprinted on Lieutenant Derek Jamison's retinas. The counter strike came in the form of a concentrated beam of light, which struck a hastily constructed barrier of earth. The dirt began to steam as the light burned it. Rocks rose from the ground to reinforce the wall of dirt, further slowing the light. In response, the light bent over the stone wall. A cry of frustration, and perhaps a twinge of pain, echoed from behind the wall.

"You all right, Ash?" John asked.

"You burnt my arm," she said indignantly.

John dismissed her injury with a wave. "It'll heal."

"I'll be sure to tell you that the next time you get a paper cut."

"Hey, paper cuts are a whole different level of pain," John protested. "How is it a tiny cut can hurt so badly? That would be the worst way to go, death by a thousand little paper cuts."

"Try giving birth," Ashley said, stepping out from behind the rock. Already the minor burn on her right arm was scabbing as the nanites worked to repair the damage. "Without pain medication."

"You had the nanites."

"A fat lot of good they did me."

"Weren't you supposed to forget that time of your life? Like giving birth? It's like a defense mechanism, you forget the pain so you don't mind having more kids?"

"I have a database in my brain." She tapped her head with her left hand. "I don't forget anything."

"There's another mammal that never forgets," John mumbled to Derek as he went to grab a bottle from the bench.

"What was that?" Ashley said, hands on her hips.

"Nothing, dear."

Ashley shook her head, stalked to her own bench and took a swig of water.

"Do the two of you always spar every day? Even when you are in space? I imagine throwing flames and light beams around in space would be...dangerous."

John chuckled. "Nah, we wrestle around in other ways aboard the *Dauntless*, but save the magic stuff for on the ground. Besides, there isn't a lot of light in the depths of space."

Derek's cheeks heated but he was curious about one thing. "You can't control the light emitted by artificial light sources?"

"It's harder," John began, "because although the light *seems* endless from an artificial light source, such as a glow lamp or ceiling light, if I draw too much energy from the source too quickly I risk burning out the light emitter. It works better when I have an entire room full of lights, then I can pull from multiple sources. Think of it like amperes when you're talking about electricity."

"I got a D in engineering," Derek said.

"So did I," John said, "a long time ago. But this is how my esteemed..."

"You mean estranged," Ashley interjected.

John quirked an eyebrow at her. "...brother-in-law explained it to me. He said a single light fixture might be the equivalent of two amps worth of current. If I draw more than that current of energy at a time, say ten amps, I will blow the fuse, extinguishing the lamp. But if I'm drawing light from ten fix lamps which are each two amps I have a total of twenty amps I can draw up to, meaning I can pew-pew more."

"You sounded smart until those last two words," Ashley said dryly. "Jason would be proud."

"You know it."

"So I presume you don't like to control indoor light," Derek observed.

"Nah, too much concentration, man. Gotta spread my consciousness around to pull in all these threads and merge them before I can output anything. It's not something I want to do unless it's an emergency. The sun, though, wee doggy the sun is limitless. If a lamp is 2 amps the sun is like a million. The current from the sun is never the problem, it's my own capacity that falters."

"And the light from fire? Such as a torch. Can you control that light?"

John shrugged. "It's the same principle. I can draw the light faster than the flame can generate it but all that does is cause a void of darkness around the flame because there's no filament or artificial source to overload. All available light from the torch is being drawn to me so none goes to anyone else. The same can happen with artificial lights if I draw right, every ounce of available light in without blowing a fuse."

"It all sounds so complicated," Derek says. "I could never be a mage."

"That's what I thought, all those years ago, my man. I was an ordinary dude, popular, on the football team, had a hot girlfriend," he pointed at Ashley. "Life was good. Then poof, there I am in a cave high up in the White Mountains, not an iota of light. We stumble around and find these trippy bracelets and put them on. *Bam*, life changed forever."

"The bracelets gave you power?" Derek asked, furrowing his brows.

"Nah, they gave us our nanites, which built the implants in our brains and let us live all this time. I don't know where the magic came from."

"My brother speculates the magic was already in us when we were back on Earth," Ashley said. "He thinks we would have developed magic on Earth naturally. Though without proper training we would have been unlikely to unlock our full potential. Either that or there was something about Tar Ebon which triggered something inside of us that was dormant. Which would mean we only developed magic because we were on Tar Ebon."

Derek opened his mouth to ask another question when movement to his right caught his eye. A young-looking man wearing black body armor approached. Ethan Edgerton. Commander of the 102nd Airborne and son of Ashley and John Edgerton.

He strode right up to his father, who had turned to face him. "Did you punch one of my soldiers?" he asked through gritted teeth.

"Ethan!" Ashley scolded. "That is no way to speak to your father."

John held up his hand upright to forestall Ashley's words. "You know the answer to that already, son," he replied coolly. "So why ask?"

"I want to know why."

"Then why didn't you say, 'hey Dad, why did you punch one of my soldiers in the face?' Why the runaround?"

Ethan clenched his fists in addition to his jaw. "Fine. *Why* did you punch one of my soldiers?"

"In the face," John prompted, making a circular motion with his index finger like a parent would to prompt a child to spit out what they were going to say.

Ethan stood silent, waiting for an answer.

Derek looked around for something, anything, he could use to distract them and de-escalate the situation.

John sighed and continued. "All right, all right, I'll tell you since you asked so nicely." He gestured back toward the temporary barracks housing the 102nd. "I was going along, minding my own business, when out of the blue this snot-nosed Marine bumps into me."

"That 'snot-nosed Marine' is a battle-hardened veteran with years of experience," Ethan protested.

Derek resisted the urge to snort. Even Marines could be pig-headed or 'snot-nosed.'

"Well that battle-hardened veteran could use a lesson in manners. As I was saying, the bugger bumps into me and instead of apologizing tells me to watch where I'm going. Now, I'm an easy-going guy," he spread his arms wide, "but I clearly had the right of way and *he* bumped into me. So I said 'I'm not the one who needed to be watching.' That didn't set well with the guy." John cocked his head to the side. "He got right up in my face and said, 'you want to say that to me again, piss-ant?'"

John shrugged. "So like I said, I'm an easy-going guy, you know it, she knows it." He gestured back toward Ashley, who was still standing near her bench. "The world knows it," he raised both arms into the air and formed a globe to symbolize the world. "Well, the world except this loser. So I said 'I'm not the one who needed to be watching. And apparently you need your hearing checked too.'"

Derek put his hand over his eyes and dragged it down his face, hiding a smile and stroking his chin.

"Then the brute's eyes went wide, his piggy face got beet red and he grabbed me by my vest. My *lucky* vest. *Nobody* touches the vest. Nobody except this mud-tromping Neanderthal with a temper, that is."

Derek wondered what a Neanderthal was but decided it wasn't the time to ask.

"So I said, 'you better unhand me before you get punched in the face.' He laughed in my face, while lifting me up by my vest. I couldn't reach my breath mints to give to him, so I punched him. In the face. Hard. He let me go, stumbled back and grabbed his nose. Before he could attack me, though, two of his buddies came up and held him back. One of the smarter ones - who knew there were smart Marines, eh, no offense, Derek - informed the bleeding beauty who I was. He went skulking off to see the medic. Does that answer your question, son?"

Ethan remained silent unclenched his jaw. "Hamilton can be a brute," he admitted at last, studying a nearby shrub bush. "But you could have just told him who you were. He would have left you alone."

"You know that's not how I roll, son. I don't like to use my title to get special treatment."

"Nevertheless, your title kept you from almost ending up laid out," Ethan pointed out.

John shrugged. "I would have gladly fought the guy, with no magic even."

Ethan shook his head. "I have to get back to my men. Just do me a favor. Next time you're walking through my camp and someone bumps into you, walk away. I don't need more men ending up hurt when the Krai'kesh are at our doorstep."

"No promises, kiddo, you know me." He gave a roguish grin.

"I wish I didn't," Ethan said in a serious tone. He turned crisply and strode away.

"Ethan Michael!" Ashley scolded again, this time striding toward him. She stopped beside John when Ethan failed to halt in response to his mother calling his name.

John's smile faded. Was he hurt by his son's words? What could he have done to cause his son to say something like that?

Ashley looked at Derek and gave a sad smile. "I'm sorry you had to witness that. He's a good boy, really. He just..."

"He's wounded," John said softly.

Derek studied the figure of Ethan as he shrank in the distance. He didn't have a limp and, while he had some scars, he didn't appear to be injured.

"Not physical wounds," Ashley said, guessing his thoughts. "Emotional scars. Scars which I'm afraid may never heal."

"You intended to tell me what happened once before," Derek began. "Are you prepared to tell the tale now?"

Ashley looked to John, who nodded. She took a deep breath before speaking. "Three hundred years ago, before the third Galactic War with the Empire, Ethan was engaged to be married to a young woman named Marie Varnes. He had dated during the centuries leading up to that point but had never been serious with any woman. He never sired children and always broke things off before the relationship became too painful."

"You mean before his girlfriends died of old age," John clarified.

Ashley nodded slowly. "He didn't have the luxury of having a mate who was as long-lived as he, like John had me and Jason had Bridgette, so he built defenses. But Marie broke through those defenses, somehow, and he fell in love, true love, for what I believe was the first time in his life. For a time, life was grand. Years passed and they were happy. They spoke of perhaps starting a family, though Marie acknowledged Ethan would likely outlive them. Nano-technology was on the horizon and Ethan believed his uncle could possibly replicate the nanite implantation process in Marie, allowing her to sire Eternal children and live as long as him. Then the war began.

"Ethan felt obligated to go to war, but made sure his fiancée, who was three months pregnant, stayed on Tar Ebon. He felt that was the safest place for her."

"And it wasn't," Derek predicted, his history lessons coming back to him slowly.

Ashley closed her eyes and shook her head. "No. During the siege of Tar Ebon, the Empire bombarded the planet for weeks. Ethan did everything he could to try to defeat the Empire and get back to his fiancée and unborn child. In the final space battle, John and I were there assisting. Ethan asked us to go down and evacuate his fiancée. He begged us, made us promise we would go get her. We of course told him we would. It was our grandchild in the girl's womb. But along the way, a battle cruiser was badly damaged and lost orbit. It plummeted toward Tera Leon and its nuclear reactor could have wiped out half of the continent of Kosh. His fiancée was halfway around the world in Tar Ebon City. We had to make a choice." Tears streamed down her face and she sobbed.

"We made the right choice," John continued where Ashley left of. "We landed in Tera Leon and I contained the explosion. The nuclear explosion which would have killed billions in an instant was instead funneled into space, destroying the Imperial flagship and causing their lines to finally break. But...it came at a cost. You see, while we were doing that, a squadron of Imperial bombers dropped bunker buster bombs on the bunker Marie was in. They weren't targeting her, instead seeking high value targets, but," John cleared his throat. A tear dripped down his cheek. "She didn't make it. If we had been there on time we could have stopped the bombs, protected her, or evacuated her before the strike happened. Ethan realized that, too, and blamed us for her death. He felt betrayed."

"But you saved billions of people," Derek pointed out. "He couldn't see that?"

Ashley shook her head. "Not in his grief. He told us someone else could have stopped the explosion and our priority should have been Marie and our grandchild. He stopped talking to us for two hundred years, traveling the edges of the galaxy in the Marine Corp as the Federation expanded. As you can see, he still hasn't forgiven us."

"I'm sorry," Derek said, feeling the word ring hollow but not knowing what else to say.

John cleared his throat and forced a smile. "Eh, it was a long time ago. But enough about us. What about you and your lady friend?"

"We've made it official. You can call Selene my girlfriend," Derek said.

"Fancy. Where is the lovely princess?"

Derek laughed. "First, she's not a princess. But to answer your question, she's up flying with your daughter's squadron."

"Ah, so how many days has she been out of your arms?" John hugged himself, crossing his arms and grabbing his back, while making a kissing motion.

Derek rolled his eyes. "Three days, I'll have you know."

"Oh, such young love," Ashley said, coming up behind John and wrapping her arms around him, interlocking her hands. For his part, he stopped hugging himself and placed his hands on hers. "Remember when we were that way?"

"Barely," John said. "Now you'd rather I sit in the other cabin on long flights."

"That is only because those ration bars don't agree with your stomach and your farts stink."

"Oh, and here I thought it was my charming personality that annoyed you."

"We were once separated for twenty years," Ashley said. "Longest years of my life."

"Eh, I kind of liked the bachelor life."

"You were in prison."

"Living the bachelor life," John reiterated.

Ashley stopped hugging John and instead slapped him in the back of the head.

"Did you do something wrong to end up in prison?" Derek asked, not being able to picture John as a criminal, despite his eccentricities.

"If you count standing up to a maniacal despot hell-bent on turning the Federation into a communist dictatorship, sure, I broke the law. At least that's what the rigged jury decided when they sentenced me to fifty years in prison."

"They knew you were an Eternal, right?"

"Of course they did. That's *why* they imprisoned me. We Eternals posed too great a threat to old Bag of Bones Billy the Betrayer."

"He likes alliteration," Ashley said dryly.

"Allita-what?" John said.

Ashley patted him on the shoulder. "Nothing, dear. Continue the story."

"So, as I was saying, we Eternals posed too great a threat. The others got away, but I wasn't so lucky."

"Why didn't you break him out?" Derek asked.

"They put him in a special facility designed to nullify magic. It was the first super-max prison of its kind to successfully replicate the nullification power previously only seen surrounding the capitol building and a few landmarks around the planet."

"So, what did you do?"

"You never heard of the Reinhart Rebellion?"

Derek pursed his lips and thought back to his history lessons. "Can't say that I have."

"Wow, what are they teaching kids these days. You know, that's why disrespectful punks like El Pig Nose act the way they do."

"Focus, dear. I swear you're getting dementia," Ashley said.

"What's that? I can't hear you without my hearing aid," John said, putting a hand to his ear.

It earned him another slap to the back of his head. Ashley sure did like to slap her husband.

"As I was saying, while I was in the slammer getting three hot meals and a cot to sleep on at night the other Eternals were on the run. Fugitives with no other planets to run to yet. They went underground, literally, and formed a resistance movement."

"They couldn't just rally the troops and depose Reinhart?" Derek asked.

John held up a finger. "Sure, they could have. Dawyn had enough clout he could have raised an army twice the size of Reinhart's. But that would have meant civil war, which would have meant the Empire pouncing like a damn cougar, which would have led to more deaths and possibly the death of the entire Federation as a government and we wouldn't be here today successfully defending against the Krai'kesh. So Dawyn and the others..."

"Mostly Dawyn," Ashley interjected. "I am not that forward-thinking."

"...decided it was best to let the usurper think he had won while planting the seeds for a quieter coup down the line. Twenty years later the plan was executed and The Betrayer was deposed."

"You'll have to tell me more of that story another time, sir," Derek said. "I have to see to my squad."

"Of course, don't let us keep you. Ash and I are heading to grab some grub."

"Err, you may want to rethink eating in the mess hall," Derek cautioned. "If 'El Pig Nose' has buddies who want revenge you could find yourself jumped and beaten down."

"See, the modern education system has failed us. It used to be attacking Eternals was understood to be a hazard to one's health. Now? Belligerent punks think they are tougher than durasteel. I'm glad we home-schooled, honey."

Ashley rolled her eyes and turned back toward the bench. "We'll go into town and get something."

Derek left the two Eternals and headed back toward the temporary Marine base. He looked up at the double moons as he did. He wondered how long the calm would last before the Krai'kesh came knocking on their door again. What surprises would they have up their sleeves this time?

Chapter 2 - Matters of Confidence

"Captain's...I mean, Admiral's log, star date October fourteen, twenty twenty-nine. We have just arrived at Yushon IV and repairs are under way. We suffered heavy casualties but the men and women of the Federation Navy were more than up to the challenge. Morale seems high, given the circumstances, but still there is a sense of the unknown which covers over things like a black cloud. Questions are being asked in corners and between bites in the mess hall about when the Krai'kesh will strike next. No, not when, *where*. I would be lying if I said that same question did not weigh on me.

"My wife and children are once again aboard my ship. They are safe and that is what matters. I have vowed to never let them out of my sight for as long as I live.

"The refugees from the Eligar system have been re-located to Yushon IV until more permanent arrangements can be made.

"The Supreme Commander is pre-occupied, managing all the ships of the Black Fleet and my own, but he seems unperturbed by the war-making capabilities of the Krai'kesh. If he's worried, he doesn't show it.

"I..." Martin stopped as his wall display emitted a ding. It indicated Zigana was calling. "Pause recording." He accepted the incoming link. "Yes, Zigana?"

"Sir, your presence is requested on the bridge immediately."

"What's happened?" he asked

"Another planet is under attack, sir."

Martin sighed. Of course. It couldn't be a notification about reinforcements, supplies or super weapons having arrived. No, it was about the Krai'kesh not being content with the minor victories, for if total annihilation of planets and making trouble for human fleets had been their goal, they had succeeded so far. "I'm on my way." He closed the link.

He arrived on the bridge minutes later and took a moment to survey his surroundings. The normal bridge crew were at their regular stations, while Zigana sat at the center, hooked up to the ship's computer via neural fiber connections. From there he had nearly any data element needed regarding the ship and its surroundings at his fingertips.

"Which planet is under attack?" he asked, taking his seat in the captain's chair.

"Proxima X, sir," Zigana replied. He brought up a holo-map of Proxima X. The planet orbited not just a sun but a gas giant, called Proxima Prime. In fact, ten planets orbited the gas giant. Technically they were moons, being only a quarter of the size of Tar Ebon. Only Proxima X was habitable, with four others covered with enviro-domes to protect the colonists from harmful radiation and the elements and the other five too unstable for even enviro-domes to be viable. Proxima X and its satellite planets lay within the Vertigo system, a sparsely populated system containing no other habitable worlds which didn't orbit the gas giant.

"What has the Supreme Commander said?"

"He asked that you contact him immediately."

"Then by all means, let's not keep him waiting."

A link was established between the admiral's ship and the *Nightblade* and Dawyn Darklance's face appeared on the holo-display. "Ah, Admiral. Did I catch you at a bad time?"

Martin frowned. A bad time? No, but why ask him that? "No, sir," he replied, letting a bit of puzzlement enter his voice. "I was recording my log but otherwise I was unoccupied."

"Good. I hate interrupting when people are busy at night. My philosophy is a war can be going on but you still need to sleep."

"I agree, sir," Martin said. Sleep had been on his mind, though he didn't correct his earlier statement

Dawyn continued, "As your tactical commander has likely informed you, Proxima X is under attack. Did he also explain the significance of that world? Strategically."

"No explanation was necessary, sir. I am aware of the deutronium mines on the planet and their value." Indeed, Martin had studied the natural resources of every planet in the sector he was assigned to. Partly out of boredom from days spent doing nothing except patrolling vacant space. Also, partly out of a desire to be prepared to make tough calls in battle depending on which strategic resources were of most value. Deutronium, needed to power much of the Federation's technology, was priceless. In fact, if it had been mere pirates attacking Proxima X the larger-than-normal defense forces would have crushed them. The corporations running the mines did not take kindly to thieves.

"Then you know we have to provide a response. What worries me, however, is the fact we are doing exactly what the Krai'kesh expect us to do."

"You think they're testing us?"

"I think their random attacks of the last several days were not so random. Instead they were likely gathering intelligence on what we value most."

"Then they can leverage that knowledge to gain the upper hand," Martin surmised.

"Precisely. As I said, we must provide a response, but we don't have to send your ship or the *Nightblade*. I expect the Krai'kesh have already moved on to another planet and we don't want to tie up either of our ships on a small mission like this."

"What are you sending in response, sir?"

"I'm dispatching the *Judicator*, support vessels, and several squads of fighters. I may also pull fighters from your fighter group to support."

"Of course, sir, what's ours is yours."

A dreadnought should be sufficient to fend off most Krai'kesh forces. "What is the status of the repairs on your ship?"

Martin looked to Zigana. He held up seven fingers, flashed them and then held up one finger. "Seventy-one percent," he said, looking again toward the display.

"Thank you, Zigana," Dawyn said dryly. "My CAG will be in touch with yours about the squadron replenishment, Admiral. Just focus on continuing the repairs and the retrofitting of your ship. We're going to need all the firepower we have if we're to avoid ruin. Meanwhile, I have to rustle up some reinforcements."

"Won't it be easy to rally reinforcements to our cause?" Martin asked.

Dawyn sighed. "I doubt it will be as easy as we both would like. Humans tend to stick their heads in the sand to avoid difficult topics. I already saw that when I told the senate the Krai'kesh had returned. Hell, I've been known to do the same from time-to-time. No doubt there are some admirals or captains with the same mentality, sad as that may be."

"Good luck then, sir."

"Thank you." He paused. "Would you care to join me, Martin? For the meeting?"

"Physically, sir, or virtually?"

"Bring a shuttle over to the *Nightblade* for this meeting, if you would."

"Of course, sir. I will be there as soon as possible," Martin said, already rising and preparing to make his way to the docking bay.

MARTIN STEPPED OFF his transport in the docking bay of the *Nightblade*. The ship really embodied the "night" feel, with bulkheads and walls painted black. Every crew member wore crisp black uniforms with the insignia of Tar Ebon on their chest.

A pair of Marines saluted him. "If you'll follow us, sir, we'll take you to the Supreme Commander's chambers," the first Marine said.

Martin nodded. "Lead the way."

They led him through winding hallways to a transport pod. It streaked along the length of the enormous ship. His own ship didn't have a transport tube - a fact he made a mental note to remedy if, no, *when*, the Krai'kesh were defeated.

They arrived at a large circular door. Two guards wearing the distinct armor and helmets of the Shadow Watch Guards flanked it. They did not turn their heads to inspect their guest. The two halves of the door separated, revealing a holo-room. The Marines left Martin and he entered.

Dawyn stood at the center of the circular room facing a terminal. He looked at it for several seconds until Martin cleared his throat. He turned. "Ah, Martin, you made good time."

"Thank you, sir," Martin replied.

"I was just about to begin the meeting." He tapped at the console and the gray panels lining the chamber transformed into the image of a conference room.

Men and women sat around an enormous circular table with space at the center. Martin and Dawyn occupied the center space. Martin could look in almost any direction, except his feet, and see some aspect of the room. *I need to requisition one of these too,* he thought. He recognized many faces from both his days at the academy and the numerous conflicts since. The Joint Chiefs were there, all four sitting in a row, while by Martin's count the entire admiralty was present.

"Ladies and gentlemen," Dawyn began. "Thank you all for coming on such short notice." He paused and his eyes swept over the members of the high command gathered there. "As I trust all of you have been briefed, our galaxy has been invaded by the Krai'kesh." He paused again, as if waiting for gasps or exclamations, but none came. These weren't senators, these were battle-hardened officers. "The Black Fleet has met the enemy in combat, with mixed success."

"Yes, Supreme Commander, it is my understanding you lost not one but two planets in the outer rim?" The question came from Admiral Bordekov. She had red hair and wore an expression which lacked any concern for the actual loss of the planets she referred to. Martin had heard all about her through the scuttlebutt.

Dawyn nodded, unperturbed by her brash comment yet still managing to show concern for the planets lost. "It is true that the Krai'kesh destroyed two worlds and rendered one uninhabitable until environmental cleanup can be arranged. They did so using gravity weapons never before encountered. We are still trying to understand the science behind it and how to counter the technology."

That was an understatement. Martin had his scientists working around the clock analyzing the data from the encounter with what was being called the "gravity drill," but still they had not been able to even create a model of how a technology like that would work. He imagined the scientists aboard the Black Fleet were having similar difficulties.

"Allow me to be blunt, sir," Admiral Bordekov's tone implied anything but respect. "Many of us have expressed concerns privately about your aptitude to lead the Federation military. What makes you the best suited to lead us against the Krai'kesh?"

Dawyn scanned the faces of the assembled admirals before responding. "Is that true? Have 'many' of you expressed concern?" No one answered. "Well, out with it. Let us discuss your concerns here and now rather than skulking in back alleys."

Admiral Varkov, a younger admiral with slicked back hair offered a greasy fake smile. "Supreme Commander, it was hardly 'skulking.' We had not had the chance to bring our concerns to you yet."

"And what concerns would that be?" Dawyn asked.

"You appointed yourself to this position two thousand years ago," Admiral Varkov said. "Back when wars were fought with sword and bow. Times have changed and, judging by the failed efforts thus far to stop the Krai'kesh, I don't think you've changed with them."

Martin blinked. Dawyn had nothing to do with when the Krai'kesh had emerged. In fact, he had come to the rescue of Martin's fleet in their darkest hour. Without the Black Fleet, countless more lives would have been lost. He opened his mouth to speak, but Dawyn shot him a warning glance and he snapped it closed.

"I will have the admiralty know that I have prepared for this day tirelessly since the day the Krai'kesh were defeated on the Fields of Pelinor. *Everything* I have done I have done for the Federation and to prepare for *this* day. So how dare you question my commitment to this cause?" His eyes were narrowed and his face scrunched up in anger. "I would expect something like this from the senators back on Tar Ebon, but from you, seasoned veterans? Bah. What examples do you point to which prove I am not fit to serve as Supreme Commander?"

Admiral Varkov did not speak, instead looking toward Admiral Bordekov. For guidance? Were their plans falling through?

"For one thing, you did not have enough military forces in the sector the Krai'kesh emerged in," Bordekov began. "For another, you allowed the Empire to remain a threat, as we are now seeing at the Imperium Line. You had a chance to crush them ten years ago and did not. That, in my mind, proves you are weak."

Dawyn pointed to Bordekov. "First, unless I had the entire Federation Navy spread out along the outer rim, leaving the mid rim and core worlds at risk for pirate raids or Imperial invasion, there was no way to ensure sufficient force was on hand when the Krai'kesh would emerge. Second, I spared the Empire ten years ago because I felt we could not risk a prolonged fight with the Krai'kesh looming on the horizon."

"Ten years is a long time for them to be looming on the horizon," Bordekov said with a sneer.

He's going to blow a gasket, Martin thought. *They're pushing him too close to the edge. Will he resign his commission?*

Instead of erupting further in anger, however, Dawyn sighed. "If you want to express your lack of confidence in me, feel free to resign your commission or defect to the Empire, Bordekov. That goes for you as well, Varkov, and any of you too scared to speak up." His eyes again swept the gathered admirals. A few averted their eyes downward - in shame?

"You misunderstand us. There is sufficient lack of confidence in your ability to lead the Federation military for us to call for a vote to decide whether you will continue to be the Supreme Commander of the Federation."

Martin blinked in shock. Could they do that? He wasn't an elected official, and his position was protected by the constitution of the Federation, much as the position of Director of the FIA was protected and held by Bridgette Thorpe.

Admiral Bordekov seemed to read Martin's mind. "And before you recite the constitution to us, know that if most of the admiralty vote no confidence in you, you will be forced to resign."

"Will you come and take the *Nightblade* from me, then?" Dawyn asked.

"We will inform your crew that you have been relieved of your command and are to be held until you may be transported back to Tar Ebon or to the destination of your choice as a private citizen. You will not be harmed - unless you resist."

Martin resisted the urge to smirk. First, the crew of the *Nightblade* were unlikely to turn on their commanding officer, the admiralty be damned. Second, even if they were to turn on him, Martin was quite sure Dawyn would not go down without a fight. The greatest warrior known to man being ousted by his crew? Not unless he allowed it.

"Then let the vote commence," Dawyn said. "Do not delay it on my account." He held up a finger. "But, the man next to me was named admiral after the admiral of this sector perished early in the Krai'kesh invasion. I expect him to have a vote."

Admiral Bordekov narrowed her eyes and glared at Martin. Was the vote so split that his vote could be the deciding vote? "Fine," she spat. "All in favor of Supreme Commander Dawyn Darklance being relieved of his command, say aye."

"Aye," came the voices of a dozen admirals.

Bordekov clenched her jaw. Not as many as she had expected, apparently.

"All those in favor of the Supreme Commander retaining his command, say nay."

"Nay," Martin said, along with fifteen other admirals. Three had not said aye or nay, and the joint chiefs were not allowed to vote.

Dawyn quirked an eyebrow. "It would seem the nays have it."

Bordekov snarled. "I will follow you no longer. Who is with me?" Her eyes raked across all the gathered admirals.

Five of the twelve who said aye raised their hands. Admiral Varkov was among them.

Dawyn nodded. "So be it. You may leave this meeting and send me your resignation in writing if you no longer have confidence in me. Am I clear?"

"You won't get away with this," Bordekov said. "You haven't seen the last of us. Your entire command is a sham, and I look forward to the day you come crashing down." She cut off her transmission without waiting for a reply. The other five who had raised their hands also cut their transmissions.

That can't be good, Martin thought. *Will they take more direct action now?*

Dawyn fell silent for a few moments. "Now that business is out of the way, are there any more concerns you wish to express concerning my position as Supreme Commander of the Federation military or can we get on with the discussion of a battle strategy?"

None of the admirals spoke. The seven who had voted against Dawyn but not resigned continued to study their virtual desks, while the fifteen others who had supported him just stared. They had done nothing wrong and had nothing to feel guilty about, other than perhaps letting the discussion get to that point in the first place. "Silence was consent" went the saying.

"Good," Dawyn clasped his hands behind his back. "As I was saying, we are still trying to understand the technology behind the Krai'kesh gravity weapon. In the meantime, we need to draw up a battle plan. Twenty-three sectors with as many fleets in addition to the Black Fleet and Home Guard. The Home Guard cannot leave," he nodded to Admiral Stephenson. "So we are left to split the remainder the best we can. My first instinct is to pull half of the fleets from the core and mid-rim sectors and move them to the invaded sector to help stem the tide. I am asking for constructive thoughts regarding this conundrum."

Admiral Stephenson cleared his throat. He wore spectacles and gray streaked his hair. "Sir, do we have a plan if the Krai'kesh attack Tar Ebon? Does intel suggest the Krai'kesh know the location of Tar Ebon?"

Dawyn chuckled and cracked a smile. "Does military intelligence ever know anything?" That elicited a nervous chuckle from the collective admiralty. His smile turned somber. "Intel, both military and FIA, knows nothing about the level of knowledge the Krai'kesh possess. Even their true motives are unclear, other than they appear to desire all of humanity destroyed. We still do not fully understand why they want us destroyed."

"I am not a politician, sir," Admiral Julia Reynolds began, crow's-feet flanking her mouth and her hair dyed a dark red, "but have we tried opening diplomatic dialog with the Krai'kesh?"

"There have been no attempts at communication with the enemy. The testimony of the Founders and the actions of the Krai'kesh on Tar Ebon two thousand years ago spoke to the futility of diplomatic solutions."

Admiral Reynolds nodded, satisfied with the answer. "I presume, sir, you have been briefed on the situation at Crossroad Station?" Her sector bordered Crossroad Station.

Dawyn nodded. "The director of the FIA gave me the limited details she had. The Krai'kesh infiltrated, our forces engaged and evacuated the Federation embassy, an Imperial and Federation fleet both arrived and things became heated. Does that sum it up?"

"Quite, sir, but the conflict there has resulted in a build-up of the Imperial Navy near the Imperium Line."

"I know. Which means we cannot move ships from those sectors," Dawyn mused. "That ties up four fleets."

"Also, sir, if the Commerce Sector truly are harboring Krai'kesh, military action may need to be taken." That from Admiral Thompson, whose fleet bordered the Commerce Sector.

Dawyn shook his head. "The FIA is working to confirm Commerce Sector involvement, but even if they are involved I do not expect you to take action against them. If we attack the Commerce Sector while still defending against the Krai'kesh the Empire will smell blood in the water and pounce or a coalition from the Non-Aligned States will try to sneak in and stab us in the side. We cannot afford to fight a war on three fronts."

"With respect, sir," he said with a tone of genuine respect in his voice, "if the Krai'kesh are found to be aiding and abetting a foreign government do we not have an obligation to respond?"

"There are other ways than force, Admiral. The president can speak to the Merchant Council and tell them to take care of it or we introduce economic sanctions or a similar diplomatic solution. I don't know all the avenues available, I am a soldier first and foremost."

"And the Empire, sir?" Admiral Reynolds asked.

Dawyn surveyed the other three admirals whose fleets bordered the Rakosh Empire's territory before meeting her eyes. "Begin conducting war games of your own. Posture and make it clear that if they attack we will be ready. In the meantime, I will ask the president to place a call to the emperor to enlist them rather than make them enemies. I would do it myself but the emperor and I do not exactly get along."

Martin snorted. Dawyn glanced his way and he straightened up. "Do not exactly get along" was an understatement, as the story went. The Supreme Commander had slammed the emperor up against a wall and threatened to run him through with his blade if he didn't call off the Iron Fleet. The emperor had wisely decided to heed Dawyn's threat, much to the relief of Martin, who had been facing said fleet. He dreamed of the Empire being on their side instead of always looming on the horizon as a potential enemy.

Admiral Stephenson spoke up. "Tar Ebon, sir?"

Dawyn shook his head. "Ah, yes, Tar Ebon. If the Krai'kesh learn of Tar Ebon's location and attack we will pull all available fleets in to assist." He held up a hand to forestall Admiral Stephenson from speaking. "Article Twelve Section Three of the Federation constitution grants an exclusion to the rule forbidding any Federation fleets other than the Home Guard enter Tar Ebon space. It can be enacted in times of grave danger which threaten the integrity of the Federation. I certainly see the Krai'kesh as a grave threat, should they show up. Does that set your mind at ease, Admiral?"

"Yes, sir, although I do wonder how the Home Guard could defend against one of these gravity weapons the Krai'kesh possess. I understand it was defeated with magic?"

"Yes, light magic."

"A magic we have no access to here, sir. The only light mage is attached to your fleet."

"As I said, we are working on a scientific solution and I also have the director of the FIA chasing a potential lead. Let us not dwell on what ifs."

Admiral Stephenson bowed in acquiescence. "Of course, sir."

"If there are no further questions, I am ordering half of the sixth, eighth, twelfth, sixteenth and twentieth fleets to our current sector to aid in military operations. That will still leave those sectors with defensive capabilities." He had not included any of the fleets belong to the admirals who had resigned their commissions. "Retrofit your fleet with as many railgun and gun batteries as possible, for those are the only weapons effective against the Krai'kesh shielding. Then proceed to the outer rim with all due haste. That will be all, ladies and gentlemen. As always, your noble service to the Federation is greatly appreciated."

The gathered admirals, including Martin, saluted and the images from the other admirals blinked out. Martin looked to Dawyn. "Well, sir, that was an... interesting meeting."

Dawyn's shoulders, which had been upright during the entire meeting, slumped. "It was disheartening seeing so many admirals lacking faith in my command. I fear how deep such lack of faith goes."

"Sir, the admirals are playing the role of rear admiral. They are not on the front lines, not seeing the existential threat the Krai'kesh pose. As more fleets face them, they will come to appreciate the gravity of the situation and respect you even more for preparing for it as best you could under the circumstances."

Dawyn gave a slight smile. "Thank you for your words, Admiral, though I do doubt the predictive nature of them. I fear that what we have is a Navy full of old yet inexperienced admirals who saw only limited combat in their careers. Training and war games can only do so much."

"That is true, sir, but the alternative would have been to engage in constant war, which could have destabilized the Federation instead of hardening it. Too much pressure can destroy even the hardest stone."

"That's exactly what my sister told me. For all her...edges...she is a prudent woman who prefers solutions other than violence. From the formation of the Federation her sole purpose has been to protect the Federation from all threats, foreign and domestic, even if that meant using methods I didn't agree with to do so. But hind-sight is twenty-twenty. I see now the things she did were often to prevent the death of more people and to prevent the Federation from becoming destabilized. She didn't always get it right, but she got us this far. One of the unsung heroes of the Federation. I am usually the one the history books tell of, but it was she, working tirelessly to keep the Federation held together, who is the real hero."

"I should like to meet her, sir."

Dawyn's expression became distant. "I expect you will, one day."

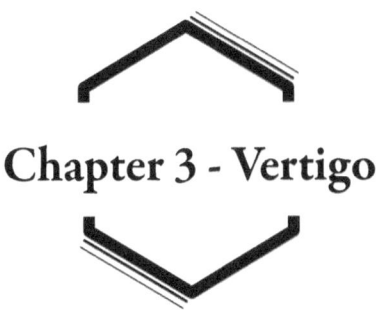

Chapter 3 - Vertigo

Selene sat in her fighter in the hangar bay of the *Judicator*, waiting to exit shadow space and emerge into an unknown situation. All communication with the system had been lost, so they were going in blind.

"How are you holding up?" Emma asked.

"You mean after you destroyed me eight out of ten times today? Humbled." More humble, really. The first moment of humbleness she felt since the arrival of the Black Fleet was being asked to join Victory Squadron. She had of course said yes.

Emma chuckled. "Hey, you should be proud of that. Most pilots don't even beat me one time. You're among the elite who have beat me twice."

"But not a record-setter?"

"Nope, that honor goes to a pilot fifty years ago who beat me five out of ten times. A savant, I swear, she was the best pilot I ever knew apart from myself."

"What happened to her?"

"She died ten years back. Old age."

"I'm sorry." She didn't know what else to say. She couldn't imagine everyone she knew, friends, family, being born, growing up and dying while she remained the same.

The line was silent for several seconds. "It happens. I'm used to it."

"At least you have your parents still, that must count for something."

Emma snorted. "When I see them. They're too busy gallivanting around the galaxy, searching for a legend."

"A legend?" Selene asked. She had spent some time with John and Ashley while aboard the *Independence*, but never heard the mention of a legend.

"Earth." She sounded disgusted. "They've been searching for the mythical planet of Earth - just Earth, mind you, not an original named world - since the first time I piloted a shuttle into space."

Selene smiled. "Was that the same day you had to be rescued by your cousin?"

Emma chuckled. "You know your history."

"I *was* educated in a noble family," Selene quipped. "And I had models of the early star ships hanging from my ceiling."

"Well, as you alluded to, that was also the day Isabelle learned she could shift outside of Tar Ebon's atmosphere. It was still centuries before shifting technology advanced, but just knowing it was possible emboldened my uncle Jason to research shifting and build a shadow drive. The rest is history." Her tone suggested it was a history she didn't always care for.

"Did you ever..." Selene was interrupted by a message from flight control both inside her cockpit and outside in the hangar bay.

"All fighters, prepare for emergence and immediate deployment. Clear all hangars. Prepare for depressurizing," the mechanical voice announced.

"We'll talk later," Emma said and the channel closed.

If we survive whatever this is, Selene thought. With details about the enemy being scarce, such as their position and numbers, it was anyone's guess as to what the Krai'kesh had planned for them.

"Emerging now," the same voice announced. The strange chilling sensation passed over her as the *Judicator* returned to real-space. "Deploying," came the voice, even as the launching mechanism in the hangar floor hurled her fighter out into space.

She oriented herself and consulted her HUD, searching for Krai'kesh signatures and preparing to take evasive action. *What in the world?* she thought.

A fierce battle ensued around Proxima X, with lasers and explosions lighting up the darkness. Several defense platforms lay in ruins, while the husks of several capitol ships floated deeper into space or plummeted toward the gas giant below.

What shocked Selene wasn't the battle. She had expected conflict. It was the signatures of those fighting. *What the Hell are they doing here?* A House Artois fleet, her family's house, faced off against a fleet of House Vivendi ships and a host of defenses.

Emma opened a channel with Selene before she could even issue the command to her implant to open one of her own. "Are you seeing this?"

Of course I'm seeing this, Selene thought. But instead of giving a sarcastic answer, as Emma was her commanding officer, she responded with a simple yes. She was still surprised seeing ships from her house so far away from the Commerce Sector.

"So much for it being the Krai'kesh. I guess intel was wrong."

"To be fair," Selene began, "we weren't told it was the Krai'kesh, correct?"

"No, the communication cut off before they could tell us who was attacking. We assumed it was the Krai'kesh. Hold on, the *Judicator's* commander is pinging me." The line went silent.

Selene took that moment to study the battle. House Vivendi's forces were on the losing end of the battle. Even as she watched another corvette went down. House Artois fighters overmatched the enemy fighters three to one.

Emma came back on the line. "Coward," she spat as if cursing.

"What's wrong?" Selene asked.

"The *Judicator's* commander is ordering the fleet to return to the Yushon system."

"Why would he do that? They need our help!"

"He says a dispute between two houses isn't his problem."

Selene's thoughts raced. "Let me speak with them," she said.

"With the commander?"

"No, with House Artois."

"Will they listen to you?"

"Probably not, but I can distract them long enough for you to figure something else out."

"All right, do it. If you're in danger, I'm coming to help you."

That's what I'm counting on, Selene thought. She punched the thrusters on her fighter and sped toward the assailing fleet. She opened a global channel and spoke. "House Artois forces, this is Selene Artois. Is a member of the Board present?"

The line remained open but silent. Finally, a male voice came over the channel. "Selene? Is it really you?"

Selene breathed a sigh of relief. It was her second-oldest brother, Frederick, rather than her eldest brother Zacharias. "Frederick, it's good to hear your voice. It has been too long."

"I heard you joined the Federation," he said. He sounded distracted.

"How did mother and father take it?" She already knew the answer and kept her eyes on the sensor display. If Emma was going to make a move she would need to do it soon.

"Mother cried for weeks on end. Father called her weak and disowned you."

All things she already knew from her own sources back home. The guilt she felt for causing her mother so much grief ate at her conscience sometimes, all those years later. "Why are you here, Frederick?"

"We're carrying out a hostile takeover. Just routine business, you remember."

She remembered. She remembered being forced to stand at her father's side at ten years old as an entire colony world was taken over by House Artois. The horrifying images of men, women and children exterminated by a combination of bio-weapons and conventional explosive ordnance shared her nightmares with the face of her mother. "So far from the Commerce Sector?"

"I'm charged with liquidating their assets, wherever they may be."

Selene snorted. Her family, and all the ruling Houses, knew how to best distance themselves from the people they hurt and killed. Invasion and genocide were called "takeovers," wholesale destruction of facilities or theft was called "liquidation." It disgusted her to think she had ever been a part of that society. "Well you've entered a war zone, brother, in case you hadn't heard."

"Oh, something about the Krai'kesh, yes?" he sounded dismissive. "We are not concerned about them."

"You'd be a fool not to." She always thought Frederick was the smarter of her two elder brothers. Perhaps she was wrong - maybe they were both idiots.

"The Krai'kesh are not concerned with us."

Selene narrowed her eyes. "How do you know what the Krai'kesh are concerned or not concerned with?"

"I just...I just meant they are not likely to be concerned with us with such a ripe target as the Black Fleet in the region."

Selene didn't buy it, but didn't have time to press her brother. A text-only message from Emma flashed across her HUD. *Keep him talking. I'm speaking to the House Vivendi forces now.*

Okay, Selene typed back. "How far are you into the liquidation process?"

"We've neutralized their defenses and are preparing to breach their facilities. Why are you asking, little sister? The commander of your task force indicated you are going to be returning to the Black Fleet."

Selene tried to think of the most House Artois thing to say. "I just want to know when you'll be done, that's all. I wouldn't want the Krai'kesh to catch you unawares."

"As I said, we have nothing to fear from the..." he stopped." What are you up to? Why is it you are communicating with us and not the commander or your squadron leader?" His voice was thick with suspicion.

Nice deflection, she thought. She sent a text-only message to Emma. *He's on to me. Whatever you're going to do, do it now.*

I heard, came the brief text a second later. The icon representing Emma's fighter, Victory One, accelerated toward the battle zone.

"What is that fighter doing?" her brother asked. All warmth had drained from his voice, replaced by a hardness akin to her father.

Emma streaked through the battle line, unchallenged by the fighters of House Artois, and reached the House Vivendi base. A blast door opened as she approached and several boxy ships exited. *Transports*, Selene thought.

"This is Commander Emma Edgerton of the United Federation of Planets. The House Vivendi fleet is now under the protection of the Federation. You will cease firing on their warships and will not attack their transports or you will face the consequences. They have agreed to evacuate."

"Bloody..." her brother began before the link closed.

"Good talk," Selene said.

For several seconds the battle continued to rage unabated, but then slowly the fighters of House Artois fell back and swarmed around their capitol ships like angry bees around a hive. Selene narrowed her eyes. If they were going to let House Vivendi evacuate, why weren't the fighters entering the hangars? She opened a channel and shouted "Emma, it's a trap!"

Too late. The enemy cruisers of House Artois fired on Emma and the cluster of transports. "No!" Selene shouted. She accelerated without thought, anger mingling with disbelief, racing toward the enemy fighters surging toward their prey like hawks diving for a hare. A quick glance at her HUD showed the rest of Victory Squadron following her. The other squadrons were hanging back.

"Victory Squadron, stand down," the voice of the *Judicator's* CAG came over the squadron channel.

"With respect CAG, that is our squadron leader."

"You are not authorized to engage. I repeat, you are not authorized to engage."

Three Victory Squadron pilots turned back. Selene kept her course as seven other fighters followed her. She wasn't sure what eight fighters could do alone, but it was better than standing by and doing nothing.

Seeing this, a new voice came over the channel. "This is Commander Dent to the remnant of Victory Squadron disobeying a direct order to return to the *Judicator*. Return now or you will face court martial for disobeying a direct order. You have one minute to comply."

"Bite me," Selene said, though the channel wasn't open. She continued her path.

"You leave us with no choice." Selene's sensors showed energy build-up in the section of the *Judicator* housing its shadow drive. Moments later it and the support ships shifted and were gone.

"Traitors!" Selene shouted, slamming her fist on the console. She opened the squadron channel. "Listen up, Victory Squadron, I don't have to tell you what just happened. We're on our own. So fight until your last breath. That's our commander out there."

"We're with you, Seven," Victory Three answered.

The remnant of Victory Squadron continued their course. Selene's HUD showed two transports from House Vivendi taking heavy damage. Emma's signature was still there, the system would have notified Selene if she were gone, but the amount of activity on the display drowned out her icon. Her fighter flashed past the flagship of House Artois. Target lock alarms blared and she did a barrel-roll, evading a hail of laser fire erupting from the flank of her brother's ship.

Did they realize their commander's sister was out there? A pair of lasers struck one of her fighters, Victory Eight, sending it veering off course. A second barrage, this time of four lasers converging on a single point, struck home and destroyed them.

Within seconds Selene and her squad were past the enemy capitol ships and closing on the rear of the fighter swarm already engaged in conflict with the transports and remaining combat craft of House Vivendi. Her first target came into missile range. Selene triggered a pair of missiles and they streaked out, curving toward the target.

The enemy fighter tried to dodge the missiles, and succeeded with the first, but the second missile struck home and the fighter exploded in a ball of short-lived flame.

Selene's next target was in coilgun range. She led her target and pulled the trigger. A thin stream of shells hurtled across the void. Several burned up in the shields, but enough passed through to damage the enemy's thrusters and send them into a tailspin. Selene's finger hovered over the trigger. Yes, she was angry at the traitors for abandoning her, her father for disowning her, and her brother for proving to be ruthless, but did this pilot, who was just following orders, deserve to die?

The decision was taken out of her hands when the fighter exploded.

So much for showing mercy.

The icon representing another Victory Squadron pilot winked out. They wouldn't survive much longer.

A ding indicated an incoming transmission. It was coming from the *Goldstar*. "I'm a little busy fighting your goons," she snapped at her brother.

"You can't win, Selene. Surrender and I assure you no harm will come to you."

"No harm until you want it to happen, you mean," Selene retorted.

"If you want to be a martyr, little sister, be my guest. I'm giving you a way out."

Selene gritted her teeth. She would be no use to the Federation dead and there wasn't a single weak point she could exploit to wreak major damage as a sacrifice. But maybe she could leverage her brother's desire for her to live. "I'll surrender if you let all the pilots in my squadron, including Emma, live as well." It would be selfish if she took him up on his offer and didn't think of them.

"But of course, little sister," he said. His greasy tone made the hairs on Selene's arm stand up but she had no other choice. "You and your fellow pilots will be my guests."

"And you'll let the remaining Vivendi employees go free?"

"Neither I nor my fleet shall harm them."

Selene switched back to the Victory Squadron channel. "This is Selene to all Federation and House Vivendi forces. I have negotiated a cease fire with the commander of the *Goldstar*. He has agreed to allow us all to live in exchange for Victory Squadron surrendering and coming aboard his ship." She left out the fact it was mostly she he wanted.

Emma, who had until that point been silent, came over the channel directly to Selene. "Do you trust your brother?"

"About as far as I can throw him, and Frederick likes his sweet treats," Selene said. "But we don't have another option, do we?"

"Not if we don't want to end up as martyrs. Fine, at least if we're alive we have a chance of escaping." She switched over to the global channel. "I concur with Selene. All Federation fighters report to the hangar of the *Goldstar* immediately. House Vivendi forces, proceed with your retreat."

The remaining fighters from Victory Squadron, now numbering six with Selene and Emma, flew one-by-one into the hangar of the *Goldstar*. No sooner had her fighter touched down than magnetic clamps locked it into place. *I guess they really don't want us to leave*, she thought. Armed guards stood around the hangar and pointed their weapons at her and the other pilots the second their canopies opened. Selene raised her hands as soon as she descended the ladder.

A gasp behind Selene made her turn. One of the pilots from her squad pointed in the distance. Void portals were opening. For a moment Selene felt a spike of hope. Had the Black Fleet come? Had word reached them somehow? But then she saw the organic prow of a large capitol ship. A *Krai'kesh* ship. She turned back to the guards. "That is a Krai'kesh ship. Tell the bridge we need to get out of here now!"

The guards continued pointing their weapons at her. "Keep your hands where we can see them and follow us," one said. "Let's go."

Why were the guards so calm about this? She had witnessed other pilots aboard the *Independence* puking when first encountering the Krai'kesh. Unless...she felt a chill down her spine. "They've seen the Krai'kesh before," she whispered.

No sooner had the Krai'kesh ships fully emerged from their void portals than they opened fire on the ships of House Vivendi. "No!" Selene shouted, stepping toward the force field protecting the docking bay from space as if she could do anything to stop them.

"Stop right there!" one of the guards shouted. A beam of light flashed past her on the right and left a burn mark on the floor inches away from her boots.

He promised he wouldn't hurt the House Vivendi forces. She hung her head as realization struck her. He had said *he* wouldn't hurt them. He'd made no mention of the Krai'kesh hurting them. She should have read between the lines, but she'd never been good at contract negotiations of the double-speak merchants used to create loopholes and manipulate others.

Chapter 4 - Hard Entry

"Oi miss Tar Ebon already," Corbin said. He sat across from Kimberly. He plucked at his uniform. "Why di' it have ta be me as the servant?"

"Because our cover demanded it," Kimberly said. "Believe me, this dress is not the most comfortable." She tugged at the hem of her dress and wiggled her toes in her white shoes."

"Oh ya, complain about playing the part of the rich merchant woman from Tar Ebon. Poor you," Corbin mocked. "Baillidh isn't even allowed in this part of the transport. He's is stuck in coach."

"I didn't know you cared so much about Baillidh," Kimberly said. *Or me*, she thought.

"Oi don't. Oi'm considering going back there if it will let me get out of this uniform."

"You have to maintain your cover. It wouldn't do to have my servant wandering around the transport."

"Well, aren' ye adaptin' to yer hoity toity role well?"

Kimberly rolled her eyes. "I wore my share of dresses back home. I guess I picked up more of the high life than I thought."

"Did ye live the charmed life of a princess?"

Kimberly snorted. "Hardly. My mother died when I was four and my father was consumed by work. But he made good money and my aunt practically raised me. She wore a dress every day and insisted girls should only wear dresses. No pants allowed in her house."

"Quite draconian."

"I didn't think so at the time. I enjoyed twirling in my dresses as a child and seeing the look on my aunt's face when I came in from outside all muddy."

"She still alive and kickin'?"

Kimberly looked down at the floor between her feet. "I neglected to mention my home planet was Galatia IV." She looked up sheepishly at Corbin to gauge his reaction.

The blank look on his face slowly changed to recognition of the name. "Oh...oh! So she...died? Did she stay dead? Is she undead? Oi ferget what the term is."

"It's undead," Kimberly replied, the face of her former best friend flashing in her mind. "But no, she died permanently and didn't resurrect."

"Oi'm sorry."

"It's going to sound callous, but I'm not sorry she died. I saw what the people who were cured went through in the aftermath of the outbreak. All the discrimination and hatred, always being looked at sideways and with poorly disguised fear in their eyes. No, I think people like my aunt and father were the lucky ones." She didn't mention the role her father had played in the infection.

"Oi've seen people from there, but never known anyone up close and personal like."

"My best friend in high school was infected. She died and rose again. It... changed her."

"Oi know oi'd be goin' crazy if oi were infected with that virus. So oi dun blame her."

Kimberly pursed her lips. There had been more to it than just the infection, but it certainly pushed her over the edge.

"How'd you survive?" he asked.

Kimberly sighed. She had expected, and dreaded, that question. "I stayed home that day with a cold. My father told me to run and hide in the woods, in a hunting blind we used to go to every fall. Going there was one of the few times I was allowed to wear pants. My aunt would tut as she saw us heading out toward the woods and usually call out how unseemly it was for a girl to be wearing pants but my father would chuckle and ignore her. That day I ran in my dress and stayed there at the hunting blind until I was rescued."

"Lucky girl," Corbin said.

"Yes. I thank the stars every day for my survival." She decided to change the topic. "What about you, Corbin? Where did you grow up?"

It was Corbin's turn to study the floor and ponder her question in silence. "Well, oi grew up in one o' them mining colonies inside the Commerce Sector. Still 'ave nightmares."

"How did you get out?"

"Me parents bribed a trader to smuggle me out. Took every dime they 'ad. They died a few years later."

"I'm sorry, Corbin." It seemed they had both lost their parents.

Corbin waved a hand to dismiss her concerns. "Bah, 'twas years ago. Oi've moved on." His clenched fists said otherwise.

"Was it in the Epsilon system?"

"Nay. Closer to the Non-aligned Planets. That's where oi went after escaping."

"How did you come to join the FIA, then?"

"Funny thing, that. See, oi fell into a life of crime, eh. Oi got in with the wrong people, yadda yadda. Ended up going to Tar Ebon for this big heist. Big, elaborate heist. So oi'm in there, stealing some bracelets a buyer is paying millions for when oi feel a rustle of wind, like a breeze blowin' through me beard. But oi' think to meself there's no windows to let a breeze in. Before oi can do much more than turn me head oi've got a knife at me throat. Know who it was?"

Kimberly shook her head, not wanting to speak and interrupt the story.

"It was the bloody director of the FIA herself, Bridgette. Holding a knife to me throat! Oi didn't know who she was at first. She asked me what oi was doin' there. Oi figured honesty was the best policy, right, and so oi told her what oi'd been sent ta steal. Know what she did next, lass?"

Kimberly shook her head again, though she felt slightly more annoyed. Obviously she didn't know what Bridgette had done next.

"She sits me down and hands me the bracelet. She tells me to go back ta the group oi was with and take the bracelet ta the buyer. So oi do, nervous as all get out. The group and oi go ta the buyer together and right after oi hand over the bracelet oi feel that same breeze. Guess who it was."

Kimberly cocked her head to the side. "Let me guess. Bridgette. Just finish the story, Corbin."

"Aye, Bridgette herself standin' beside me! The goons oi was with weren't too happy ta see her, though, and they decided ta attack her. Fools. She made short work of 'em and soon had the buyer on his knees as FIA agents and security forces swarmed the place. Afterward, she comes over ta me and asks if oi want a job in the FIA. O' course oi couldn't refuse. So oi joined up and the rest be history."

"Impressive story. Did you ever figure out what the buyer wanted with the bracelet they were willing to pay so much for it?"

"She didn' tell lowly ol' me, mind you, but the group that got me in there ta steel it said it had some magical powers of immortality or something. The buyer wanted ta see if the claims were true."

"While I know magic exists, I doubt a bracelet could make someone immortal."

"It was in that vault for some reason, lass."

She couldn't argue with that, so instead settled for looking out the viewport at the planet they were fast approaching. Epsilon III boasted a large metropolis which dominated the east and west coast of the primary continent. The center of the continent appeared sparse. "They have a feudal society, right?"

Corbin followed her gaze. "Aye, there is no middle class in the Commerce Sector. Yer either wealthy or working poor. The working poor be in so much debt they never get out of it by working. That's why so many men and women become mercenaries - they want a chance ta become something more by piggy-backing on the success of the merchant families or corporations."

"Sounds depressing."

"Eh, on the mining base most people indulged in pleasurable activities ta forget their shitty lives. Oi was called crazy fer wanting to leave."

"Five minutes to landing," a voice came over the intercom.

"'Ave you talked to the ambassador yet?" Corbin asked.

"He strikes me as a lecherous old man." Indeed, he had stared openly at her when she was boarding the ship, his beady eyes looking her up and down. It had sent a chill down her spine.

The ship touched down a few minutes later and Kimberly departed the ship, Corbin following obediently behind her. They stood to the side and waited for Baillidh. He trotted down the ramp with a backpack as his only luggage.

"How was coach?" Corbin asked.

"Uncomfortable. I sat next to a woman who snored the entire time. Hard to concentrate."

"Where to next, your highness?"

"I'm a merchant, not royalty, Corbin."

"'ere they're pretty much the same thing. At least for the big merchants in the Commerce Sector."

"Well I'm a foreign merchant, so I doubt it will apply to me."

"Eh, fake it till ye make it."

"Fake it till I become a snobby merchant?"

"If we want ta survive here, yeah."

"Do snobby merchants slap their insolent servants?"

"Careful, lass, oi might like that."

Kimberly rolled her eyes and turned to their destination. The transport was docked on an outdoor landing pad connected to a private facility owned by AstCorp. A prominent logo incorporating an asteroid loomed above the entrance. "Are there no public facilities here?"

"No, ma'am," Corbin responded. "No welfare or social services. Ye lose yer job and the government won't help ye."

"So what do those people do?"

"Some will go to loan sharks and become indentured servants. Others will become beggars on the street. Still others sell themselves into slavery ta have a roof over their head and food in their bellies."

"It sounds so brutal," Kimberly said.

"It's that there trickledown economics at work. The top gets everything and the bottom gets very little. Yer house can burn down here if ye don't pay the local corporation that owns the fire department."

"Let's hope we're not stuck here, then."

"Aye."

The ambassador from the Federation, Archelaus Barrius, strode off the transport, nose up in the air and a haughty expression on his face. He ogled Kimberly as he passed but refrained from speaking to her. Kimberly smiled politely at him, even as she imagined kicking him in the groin. She and the two men followed the ambassador and his cloud of hangers-on and assistants into the AstCorp facility where a security checkpoint was set up. "Let me guess, private security forces?"

"Private thugs is more like it. Count yer valuables after going through a checkpoint like this. They'd sooner steal yer stuff and beat ye up if ye call them out than look at ye."

"Speaking from experience?" She understood his bitterness after being oppressed living in the Commerce Sector, but for him to know about the thuggish nature of security forces on the capitol planet she guessed it came from first-hand experience.

"Oi just know their kind. Every corporation employs the same handful o' security contractors who dole out these mercenaries masquerading as security forces."

"Maybe they'll be on their best behavior since we're with the ambassador," Kimberly suggested.

It turned out they were not on their best behavior. "Name?" a hulking guard asked, glaring at Kimberly as she passed. Maybe he was angry about processing so many passengers at once. Had they interrupted his lunch break or something?

"Evonne Sommrich," Kimberly replied, reciting the name displayed on her passport which she had memorized on the journey to the Epsilon system. She resisted the urge to fidget and hoped she wouldn't break out into a sweat. The best techs in the FIA had forged her credentials and proliferated the details onto the Shadownet, yet there was still a chance her cover could be blown. Would the ambassador intercede on her behalf if she were caught? No, Isabelle said they were on their own. If they were caught with falsified credentials they would be captured, interrogated and imprisoned for a long time. She swallowed hard.

The man held her passport up to a scanning pad. For several seconds nothing happened, then finally it flashed green. He shoved it back at her, almost causing her to drop it. "You're clear to enter."

Kimberly bowed her head. "Thank you, sir." The action elicited a surprised expression from the guards, followed by a narrowing of his eyes. Crap, she forgot merchants didn't say thank you to lowly security guards, let alone show deference by referring to them as sir. More words wouldn't help the situation, so instead she dropped her passport back into her bag, looked straight ahead and passed through the body scanner, head held high and back straight. *Fake it till you make it, fake it till you make it*, she repeated in her mind. No alarms went off and she turned to watch Corbin and Baillidh passing through. Baillidh got through without any problem.

"Did they take your datapad?" she whispered.

"No, ma'am," he replied in a whisper.

"Maybe Corbin was telling a tall..." she stopped at a commotion at the scanning station.

"Get yer hands off me!" Corbin shouted. "Ye ain't stealing me stuff."

Kimberly raised her hand to slap it against her face but then remembered his fake position and settled for clenching her fist at her side. She approached the station, or as close as she could come without passing through the body scanner and shouted, "Is there a problem with my servant?"

"This guy's tryin' ta steel my cred-card," Corbin said indignantly. He glared at the security guards, who seemed unaffected and exhibited no remorse.

"Move along," the guard growled. "Or else."

"Corbin," Kimberly warned. The last thing they needed was Corbin being thrown into a back room to rot for a while. "Apologize to the guard and get moving. I have places to be."

Her haughty tone snapped Corbin out of his anger. He gave her a sheepish glance, whether real or fake it didn't matter, and bowed. "Yes, ma'am." He turned to the guard. "Oi apologize for the false accusation. Sir." The "sir" came out as if he were being asked to eat something slimy and horrible smelling.

The guard glared at Corbin, perhaps still considering making his life a living Hell. But after several tense seconds he handed Corbin's passport back. "Move along," he repeated.

This time Corbin did not argue. He passed through the body scanner and joined Baillidh on the other side. Kimberly strode up to him and slapped him, part for show and part out of real anger. What had gotten into his mind that would cause him to act in such a way when the stakes were high? She told him as much. "Fool! I'm docking you a day's pay for that stunt. Pray I don't punish you further."

Corbin bowed his head but gave her a hooded glare, communicating his lack of appreciation for her *faking* it. "Yes, mistress," he said.

Kimberly turned and walked in the direction the ambassador's retinue had gone. She saw them in the distance near the exit of the docking facility. She walked as fast as she could while wearing high heels.

A line of hover-limousines waited when they passed through the doors and entered the outside once again. The air smelled...clean. Too clean. It smelled sanitized in a way her home planet or even Tar Ebon never had. *It smells fake*, she thought. *Like they're trying to pretend dirt and trash and grime don't exist. Living in their own utopia built on the backs of the poor.*

One limousine driver held a holo-sign with "Miss Sommrich" flashing.

Kimberly stopped in front of the door to the limousine. Corbin was walking around the other side of the limo. Kimberly cleared her throat.

Corbin stopped and looked at Kimberly. "What?"

Kimberly widened her eyes, looked toward the limo door and tilted her head.

"Oh, sorry m'lady. Oi'm a bit slow," he explained to the limo driver. He came around the limo and opened the door for Kimberly.

She did not thank him, instead entering the limousine in as stately a manner as possible. Baillidh and Corbin entered on the other side and sat across from her. She motioned for him to close the glass between them and the driver. "For all your talk of faking it, Corbin, you're doing a poor job."

He lowered his voice. "Maybe it's part of me plan, lassy. Make everyone thing oi'm a half-wit."

That was surprisingly brilliant. If anyone was keeping tabs on her retinue they might be watching their every move. She looked out both side windows and the back window, as if spies would be so obvious. "Baillidh, can you detect any bugs or electronic surveillance on us?"

Baillidh looked up from his datapad. "I've already scanned for bugs. We're clean. As for electronic surveillance, there is so much signal saturation here I can't tell what is directed at us or not. I'm recording the data, though, and if we're being monitored I should be able to isolate the signal as we move."

"That's better than nothing," Kimberly said.

The limousine jerked as it glided away, following the rest of the ambassador's retinue. The plan was to arrive at the embassy, get their bearings and register as Federation citizens traveling abroad as expected and then rendezvous with the resistance forces. Advance communication with the resistance was forbidden, they would have to knock on their proverbial door and speak with them. Twenty minutes later the limousine came to a halt as it waited in line for the Federation embassy to let them in. Each limousine in the line passed through a vehicle scanner and presumably the identities of the occupants was confirmed. The ambassador's vehicle passed through quickly, while the rest were subjected to higher scrutiny. When it was their turn the driver rolled down the windows of the limo. Kimberly felt exposed, even though she was entering Federation soil.

"Name?" the Federation guard asked. He wasn't as gruff as the private security fellow had been, but he was all business.

"Evonne Sommrich," she replied. "Merchant from Tar Ebon. These are my servants." She offered her passport and prompted Corbin and Baillidh to surrender theirs.

The guard checked each of the three for several seconds before handing them back. "Clear to enter," he said, slapping the top of the limo to signal the driver.

Inside the gates the limos lined up around the circle drive in front of the embassy. The building was modeled after older Tar Ebon architecture, with white marble pillars holding up the overhanging roof before entering the white embassy building. A flurry of activity ensued as porters carried luggage and other supplies into the building. The ambassador strolled up the steps, ignoring the bustle around him. He didn't have to fake it.

"Let's get inside and get settled," Kimberly said aloud, though both men likely remembered the plan still. "Then we'll seek out our friends." Her feet were hurting her already, but she hadn't brought a change of clothing. She'd have to go shoe shopping before tromping out to meet the rebels.

Chapter 5 - Fire in the Deep

"Sir, the *Judicator* has returned."

"Ah, good." No news was good news in this case. They had received no word from the fleet requesting aid.

"We're receiving a broadcast from the *Judicator*, sir."

"Probably to report the good news. Let's hear what they have to say."

"This is Commander Dent to Fleet Command. I have casualties to report."

Casualties? Martin thought. "Zigana, how many support ships did they leave with?"

"The same number as they have now, sir."

Commander Dent went on, "During operations in the system we were ambushed by the Krai'kesh. The fleet was able to escape mostly intact. However, Victory Squadron performed a rear-guard action to allow for our escape. There were no survivors."

Martin stared out the viewport in shock for a moment, not believing his ears. No survivors? Several of his pilots had been promoted to Victory Squadron temporarily. "Zigana, call up the list of our pilots in Victory Squadron."

"Of course, sir."

"Supreme Commander, I request permission to come aboard and speak with you about this matter in person."

The link was silent for a moment. Was the Supreme Commander in as much shock as Martin? Surely not, he had seen hundreds, perhaps even thousands, more lives lost in battle over the centuries. Even for Martin it wasn't the loss of life which hit hard, pilots and soldiers sometimes died in war. No, it was the suddenness of losing an entire squadron.

"Permission granted," Dawyn replied.

"Sir," Zigana began, puzzlement in his voice. "I was searching for signs of hull damage or decreased shield integrity as a result of Krai'kesh weapons but am unable to detect any. Also, my connection to the returning ships is being blocked."

Martin furrowed his brows and looked to Zigana. "Blocked? By who?"

"The Tactical Commander of the *Judicator*, sir."

"Can they do that?"

"It is against Federation regulation R262 but it is technologically possible."

"Can you break through the block?"

"Given enough time, sir, yes."

"Do it." A suspicious feeling took hold in his stomach. They had just had near mutiny among the admiralty. Could the animosity expressed during the meeting of the admirals have spread that quickly? Or had it already been festering? No, they were jumping to conclusions. They had no evidence of wrongdoing on the part of the *Judicator*. Not enough to accuse them of betraying their own.

A shuttle launched a minute later from the *Judicator* on a path to the *Nightblade*. It had no sooner docked than a signal originated from the *Judicator*. "For the glory of Rae!" Commander Dent shouted. A reddish-orange burst of flame erupted from the hangar bay of the *Nightblade* and pieces of the hull flew out into space.

Shit, Martin thought. "Raise shields!" he snapped at Zigana. "Activate weapons and target the *Judicator* but hold fire until I say. Launch all fighters." The pieces were starting to click together in his mind. A returning fleet which had run into Krai'kesh resistance but received no damage, no other casualties other than Victory Squadron reported and the *Judicator's* Tactical Commander blocking Zigana.

Target lock alarms sounded as dozens of missiles erupted not just from the *Judicator* but several ships in its battle group and others scattered throughout the fleet. Had everyone gone mad? The *Judicator* activated its engines and moved on a direct intercept course toward the *Nightblade*. A chill went up Martin's spine. He had no other choice. "Focus fire on the *Judicator*. Order our fighters to form a screen. Nothing gets close to us, not fighters or transports. We don't know who we can trust."

A blast sounded behind him, followed by a surprised grunt and a thump. Martin turned to see one of the Marines who had been flanking the door pointing his rifle at Martin, while the other Marine lay on the floor unmoving. "Order the shields lowered and recall your fighters."

Martin gritted his teeth. Traitors aboard his own ship? He didn't remember the Marine's name so he tried a different tactic. "Why are you doing this?"

"The god-emperor Rae commands it," the Marine recited, as if by rote.

God-emperor? "I've never heard of him." His hand drifted toward his sidearm.

The Marine shook his head. "I wouldn't do that if I were you. You will hear of the god-emperor soon enough. He comes and with Him comes glory for those who worship Him."

Martin rolled his eyes and shook his head but moved his hand away from his sidearm. "All right, let's say your god-emperor is real," he paused as the Marine lifted his rifle in warning. "Okay, your god-emperor *is* real." *In his head*, he thought. "Where is he?"

"He crosses the void as we speak. But His harbingers have come to prepare the galaxy for His return."

Martin frowned. There was a lot to read into in that statement. Crosses the void? Return? That implied he had been there before. Unless... "He's a Krai'kesh?" he asked in disbelief.

The Marine snorted. "Fool. He is far beyond a mere Krai'kesh. He is the god-emperor of the Krai'kesh, the one who created them and who rules them."

"So, still related to the Krai'kesh."

"You know nothing, Captain Rigsby. Enough stalling. Lower your shields and recall your fighters."

Martin looked at the sensor display. The *Judicator* was nearing the *Nightblade*, which looked to have lost a good portion of its starboard side to the vacuum of space. What kind of ordnance had they used? They had to stop the *Judicator* before it rammed the *Nightblade* and finished the job.

Zigana, Martin said through his implant. *Can you notify security?*

I already have, sir. The master-at-arms is mustering a team, but they are concerned about casualties among bridge crew, including you, should they try to breach.

We're going to have a lot more casualties on our hands if we lower the shields.

I understand, sir. The master-at-arms is determining the best method of breaching. There is also the matter of betrayal in other areas of the ship. A group of sailors were caught trying to raid the armory after the broadcast went out. Their plan was foiled, but the crew are on high alert and tensions are high.

I'll try to keep him talking a little longer. "You're willing to die for a god you've never seen or met? A god that rules over another race? What benefit does that give you?"

"I would not expect the unenlightened like you to understand, but we have been promised everlasting life for our service to the god-emperor."

"And that is a promise religion has been making for thousands of years," Martin said. "It's not exclusive to this god-emperor of yours. What guarantee do you have that he will follow through?"

"The Book of Rae tells of His coming. It has foretold this invasion and speaks the truth about the past."

"Oh really?" He would have to get his hands on that book...if he didn't get shot first.

The Marine looked at the sensor display. "You're stalling." He lifted his rifle up and thrust it toward Martin. "Lower the shields." He pointed his rifle at one of the sensor operators, Sandra. "Unless you want to lose your crew one-by-one."

"What is your plan, Marine? To die a martyr?"

"I do what is required for the glory of Rae. Even as we speak our plans are being carried out on this ship and across the fleet. Rae's will shall be done."

What a fanatic.

Sir, a security team is staging outside the door to the bridge. I am going to open on their command.

Martin kept his expression neutral. *Do it.*

"Well, I hate to tell you this but," he paused as the door to the bridge slid open.

The Marine spun, but before he could fire a shot four energy beams slammed into him, melting his armor and burning into his flesh. He screamed, dropped to the floor, and stopped moving.

Martin nodded to the Master-At-Arms, Boden Moss. "Thank you, Master-at-Arms."

Boden nodded to him. "Just doing my job, sir. The brig is starting to fill up with traitors. There have been a few casualties. I have men I can trust guarding critical infrastructure such as engineering and munitions. It appears the extent of their plan was to wreak as much havoc as possible when the broadcast came through."

"Well, they certainly caused some havoc, but it could have been much worse. Please see that all the wounded are treated as soon as possible." He focused on the fallen Marine for a moment. He was not breaking.

Martin turned back to the sensor display where the *Judicator* was taking heavy damage as the *Nightblade* and a few other Black Fleet ships fired on it but the gap was narrow. Even as Martin watched the *Judicator* plowed into the *Nightblade*. Explosions rumbled through the interior of the ship, spreading outward as the *Judicator* crumbled against the hull. Then the unthinkable happened. The *Nightblade* split in two.

"Abandon ship, abandon ship," came the call from Dawyn.

Shit, Martin thought. "Dispatch transports for rescue operations. Try to find the Supreme Commander. Order our fighters to provide protection. How many more ships have gone rogue?"

"I am trying to discern the exact number, sir. Missiles and projectiles are flying in every direction. Two ships have targeted us but not fired yet."

"I hate not knowing who we can trust. Fire on anyone who fires on us first or that we can verify has gone rogue."

"Yes, sir."

At that moment, the front half of the *Nightblade*, the portion which contained the bridge, exploded.

DEREK SAT WITH HIS squad in the mess hall munching on stale, dry chips when the talking died down and whispering began. *What's going on?* he thought.

He caught a word, "Victory," and thought there may have been a victory against the Krai'kesh he missed. But then he heard "Victory Squadron." That was the squadron Selene had transferred to. He stood up and walked to where the whispers had originated. A Marine wearing the insignia of a communication officer stood there. "What's this about Victory Squadron?"

"I overheard some chatter saying Victory Squadron was lost during a recent mission," he replied.

Derek felt a chill down his spine and a lump in his throat. "And you're sure?"

"Positive. Heard it myself."

Derek turned, numb, and walked past where his squad indulged in their own unappetizing meals.

"Sir?" one Marine asked.

Derek didn't answer. *Selene.* He wandered out of the building and focused on walking. It couldn't be true. They had just begun to have a real connection and the universe had to take her away from him? Then another thought hit him. Had John and Ashley been told? How would they take the news their daughter was dead?

His comm came to life as it received a broadcast signal. "For the glory of Rae!" a male voice shouted, then the link closed.

That was an odd thing to say. Who's Rae?

Moments later he heard laser fire coming from the mess hall. He spun and raced inside, drawing his sidearm as he went. A horrifying scene met him inside.

Tables were upturned, lasers streaked across the mess, unarmored Marines took cover. One ran for the exit but dropped as a laser took them in the back. Derek leapt behind a table and activated his internal comm. He switched it to the squad channel. *What the hell happened?*

Sir, the sergeant said, *the message about some guy named Rae came through all our implants and then several Marines started going ballistic. We're targeting anyone who is targeting us, but we still don't know who the friends and foes are completely.*

Shit. Some kind of trigger word?

Unsure, sir.

All right, fall back, we've got to get back to the Dauntless.

Yes, sir.

"Grenade!" someone in Derek's squad called out loud. An explosion came seconds later from in front of Derek, the shrapnel making a thunk noise as it slammed into the table he hid behind.

Covering fire, the sergeant ordered. Three Marines from his squad rose and fired with their sidearm at anyone who was firing in their direction while a cluster of their squad-mates made for the door. They hadn't been prepared for insurrection and as so didn't have their rifles or armor. A laser hit one of the Marines in the leg and he limped along. Two other Marines stopped to help him.

I'll cover you, Derek offered, rising and firing toward a pair of traitorous Marines firing in the direction of his squad-mates. One lucky bolt hit one opponent in the head. The enemy fire ceased as the second enemy stopped and ducked down to check on his fallen comrade.

The three Marines crouched low and ran for the exit. Derek followed at last, zig-zagging as he ran to make himself a harder target. No return fire came.

Outside Derek met up with the rest of his squad. The scene outside looked much like inside the building. Smoke billowed up from multiple directions, casting a gloom over the camp. Explosions echoed in the distance, laser fire sounded all around. His squad was once again facing enemies, this time hiding behind an APC and several other hovercrafts.

They had to get back to the *Dauntless* and gear up. Or the armory. He looked toward the north but the densest smoke rose in that direction. Who was in control of it? They didn't have much choice, however, for the *Dauntless* was parked in the center of an open field with no cover for miles around. They would be easy targets for anyone with advanced weapons. They needed to hit the armory first. *Squad, we're going toward the armory. Northward.*

The entire squad moved in a leapfrog pattern from behind the vehicles to behind pre-fabricated buildings and then to whatever cover they could find as they went. They didn't always encounter enemies, but they watched each Marine they spotted with suspicion. Several groups of hostiles attacked them. Some carried only their sidearm, but others carried rifles or grenade launchers and tried to target Derek and his squad. One of his men fell to shrapnel from a grenade, prompting another Marine to pick him up and carry him.

They neared the armory and found it being defended by a group of Marines. *Are they the good ones or the bad ones?* Derek thought. Beams of light lanced out and coilgun shells streaked through the air as the firefight continued. A figure covered in black armor strode out the main entrance. Several beams of light streaked toward him but reflected off an invisible shield of some sort. He then hurled a ball of fire in the direction of the fire and it expanded as it went, becoming a wall of fire, which engulfed his enemies. Derek recognized the symbol on the chest of the armor - Ethan.

Fire on the enemies outside the armory. The good guys are inside. He suited action to words by taking aim at the back of several enemies and firing. Before they realized they were under attack from behind they had lost several men. They retreated in the opposite direction from both Derek's squad and the armory. Once the coast was clear Derek approached the armory, where several Marines were emerging.

Ethan nodded to him as he approached. "Lieutenant, it's good you survived."

Derek saluted. "Sir. What the hell is going on?"

Ethan shook his head. "I don't have enough intel yet, but circumstantial evidence suggests the soldiers who betrayed us were sleeper agents in the service of whoever Rae is. I've seen insurrection before, even coordinated insurrection like this, but never at this magnitude. It was fortunate my men and I were on patrol in this sector when the signal came through. We heard weapons fire and saw a large group of men heading toward the armory. When we went to intercept them, they fired on us. Their mistake, but then more came while we were gearing up."

"It's widespread, then?"

"At least in this system. It's a mess in orbit - ships fighting ships, high explosive ordnance detonated inside the *Nightblade's* hangar and now she's about to be rammed."

"We need to get to the *Dauntless*."

"I agree." Ethan looked around. "I wish I could do more."

"Did you...did you hear about Emma?"

"She's not dead," Ethan said, confidence in his voice. "The commander who reported her death minutes later betrayed the Federation. We can't trust his testimony. She may be stranded somewhere or captured, but she's not dead, yet. But that's even more reason to reach the *Dauntless* and head to her last known location." He activated his internal comm and broadcast on the Marine frequency. *Attention all Federation Marines still loyal to the Federation. Stand and fight, then rendezvous at the transports and get off-world. To the usurpers, the traitors, know this: never in two thousand years of the Federation has an insurrection succeeded for long. You are on the losing side, and I will show no mercy to you. Pray this Rae has mercy on your souls.*

He switched back to the channel encompassing his own and Derek's squad. *Okay teams, we're heading to the* Dauntless.

The two squads of Marines made their way to the *Dauntless*. Explosions and the zap of laser fire continued to sound in the distance. Overhead two star-fighters engaged in a dogfight. It didn't last long - one soon defeated the other.

The *Dauntless* came into view, but the sight made Derek quicken his pace. A group of enemies were attacking the ship. A propelled grenade sailed through the air and exploded against the shields. A laser cannon on a tripod hammered at the shield with rapid beams of energy. How much longer would the shields hold out?

These enemies were not caught as unawares. Several pointed toward where Derek and the squads were oncoming and they turned to face them. A grenade sailed through the air. Instead of impacting on the ground, however, it sailed to the north, likely from Ethan using magic to deflect it. Next came a hail of lasers, which impacted against an invisible force as they had before at the armory, like rain on an umbrella. Forget the *Dauntless*, how long would he hold out?

They reached rifle range and laid down suppression fire. Derek withdrew a grenade of his own. "Ethan!" he shouted. "Give this a boost!" He tossed the grenade high into the air, hoping it wouldn't fall on him and explode. Fortunately for him Ethan heard him and the grenade went sailing through the air. It exploded on the laser-mounted tripod, sending the two Marines operating it flying. They did not get up.

"Cover me!" Derek shouted. The friendly fire increased as his squad redoubled their efforts. He ran forward, drawing his blade as he went. A figure beside him caught his eye. Ethan ran beside him. Two stray bolts of energy streaked toward Derek but were absorbed by a shield. As he neared the enemy he recognized several of the men. They were the ones who had confronted John earlier that day. What a coincidence. He targeted the big Marine who had gotten in John's face, getting ready to run him through.

The enemy Marine prepared himself by drawing his own blade. He let out an evil-sounding laugh.

Derek swung his blade down but his strike was parried by the enemy's blade. The enemy Marine moved fast for being such a hulking man and countered with rapid strikes which caused Derek to stumble back and almost fall to the ground. He caught himself but barely managed to parry the next thrust from his opponent. Damn this guy was good. He was stronger than Derek. Derek dodged the next side swipe and swept out his own blade toward the hulking man's legs. The blade impacted the armor but didn't pierce it.

His opponent brought his blade down but Derek leapt to the side, narrowly missing a sword hitting his head. Then he lifted his blade and blocked the next strike. He pushed against the blade that wanted his blood with all his strength, muscles straining, motors in his armor squelching in protest. If he lost, if he gave in, if his strength gave out, he would die. Moments passed as he struggled against the superior strength of his enemy. He didn't even have the strength to speak, to taunt his enemy. All he could do was grunt with the strain.

Relief came when flame engulfed the man he crossed swords with. The searing heat penetrated his armor but the large man, being the primary victim, screamed in pain and waved his sword around wildly. Derek leapt back to avoid a stray strike but did not go in to fight further. Instead he panted in relief and looked for the source of the flaming strike.

Ashley Edgerton stood midway down the ramp of the *Dauntless*, waves of heat blurring her image. They must have lowered the ramp during the distraction Derek and the others caused. She cast out her hands and the air in front of her ignited. She formed it into another ball of flame and threw it toward where another two enemy Marines were still firing toward the reinforcements. The ball exploded between them and their armor ignited.

By this time the remaining Marines in Derek and Ethan's squads had begun their advance. The enemy Marines must have recognized they were losing but still did not surrender.

I want one alive! Ethan commanded through the link. *Preferably two.*

It might be a little late for that, Derek thought, though he kept it to himself. Many of their opponents were dead, but they might be able to find some wounded but unconscious to capture. His eyes drifted again to the two struck by the fireball. They had probably not been killed by the fire. He approached where they lay limp on the ground. He deactivated the helmet of the first Marine and scanned for a pulse.

Faint. He checked the second Marine. *Stronger but also faint. I've got two over here*, he said through the link.

Derek heard shouting and turned to see Ethan ordering a traitor to stand down and surrender. Instead the man withdrew a grenade and stuck it in his mouth. Derek turned his face away to avoid seeing what he knew would come next. These men would rather die than surrender or be captured? They would have to watch the two they had managed to capture.

If you fellas are done out there, get aboard so we can take off, John said through short range broadcast to the group.

The Federation Marines walked, limped, or were carried aboard. The two prisoners were hauled aboard as well. Ethan was the last up the ramp, Derek at his side. Ethan paused, turned, and looked back toward the Marine base which was now in turmoil and ruin. "Such a shame," he said softly before entering the *Dauntless*.

Derek stopped by the makeshift brig to make sure the traitors were secure. He ordered all their armor be removed and they be thoroughly scanned and searched for any suicide implements or tracking devices. Then he made his way to the bridge. John was in the pilot chair, Ashley at his side in the co-pilot chair. Ethan was nowhere to be seen. Derek cleared his throat. Surely they had heard about Emma? "About your daughter..."

John waved a hand. "Eh, at first we shed some tears. Okay, I'll be honest, I was bawling like a baby. But then that strange order about Rae comes down and all hell breaks loose with the very fleet which pronounced my daughter dead turning out to be traitors. Nah, I don't think she's dead."

"But she is in trouble," Ashley said. "We have to find her. She could be captured or stranded and about to be killed."

Were they trying to convince themselves their daughter was still alive or did they truly believe she was? Derek had to admit they had a point in that the word of traitors could not be trusted. But if she hadn't returned, what had happened to her? "Where are we going next, then?"

"Going to rendezvous with the *Independence* and then go to the system Emma was last seen. Try to find some clues."

"Sounds like a plan." Derek took a seat at the sensor station. Just then an alert flashed up on the screen. The long-range sensor array had detected new contacts. "Shit," Derek swore.

"Shit is right," John said, pulling up the sensor feed on the main display. "We've got a lot of Krai'kesh contacts. There go our plans of skipping town right away." He started up the engines and began his pre-flight check. "But we have to get up there to fight. Hang on."

Yes, Derek thought. *Hang on, Selene. I won't abandon you.* He didn't even know if she was still alive either and he was avoiding thinking about the matter. Some part of him knew it was hypocritical to criticize the Edgerton's for their optimism while being equally optimistic, or in denial, about the survival of his own beloved.

"NO," MARTIN WHISPERED as the light from the *Nightblade's* explosion shone into the bridge. The Supreme Commander. Could he...did he...die? "Prioritize the Supreme Commander, Zigana. If he's alive, we must find him."

"Of course, sir, but we are detecting multiple void portals," Zigana reported. He paused. "Krai'kesh signatures."

Damn. Could their day get any worse? There couldn't have been worse time. He slapped his forehead. "Of course, the traitors are working with the Krai'kesh. That's the only explanation. How many ships can we trust, Zigana?"

"I have extrapolated the firing data, sir. Based upon how many ships have fired on us and which ships have fired on them and cascading outward I estimate twelve cruisers, twenty destroyers and thirty-two corvettes remain loyal to the Federation. Those numbers are dropping, however, as ships are destroyed. Captain Yamaguchi's ship has been destroyed."

"Damn it. What about our ground forces?"

"We lost contact with our ground forces shortly after the signal went out from the Commander. Sensor data reflects a larger than normal number of explosions and energy output on the surface and in the atmosphere."

"So our Marines are fighting for their lives too."

"It would seem so, sir."

"Order all remaining ground forces to return to the fleet. Also advise the planetary government to issue evacuation orders. We will take on any civilians who can get here before we retreat. We may need to leave in a hurry." He eyed the emerging Krai'kesh ships. They boasted at least as many ships as remained loyal to the Federation. Add the traitor ships to that number and the loyal ships were outnumbered almost two to one. He noticed a larger than normal void signature on the display. He pointed to it. "What is that, Zigana?"

Zigana furrowed his brows. "A massive ship is emerging, sir. Sensors are estimating its size as four times as large as the *Independence*. Its features match that of the Krai'kesh vessels."

"Bloody hell." How were they going to fight something like that? They had to, if only to buy time for the ground forces to evacuate.

The massive Krai'kesh ship wasted no time. It accelerated toward the *Spirit of Zion*. The loyalist cruiser fired missiles, rail-gun and coilgun munitions at the large ship but everything was absorbed. It reminded Martin of how the planet-busting gravity ship had defended itself. Nothing short of magic, and maybe not even that, would pierce that shield. When it was a few thousand kilometers from its target a beam of warped space, which appeared to the eye as darkness, connected the giant ship with the *Spirit of Zion*. No sooner had the beam connected than the *Spirit* began to shake. Pieces of ship flew off into the void. Garbled communication came through the link but it was unintelligible. The *Spirit of Zion* exploded as the gravity beam ruptured the power supply of the vessel. For a moment orange and red flames expanded outward before being sucked into the gravity beam. The pieces of the ship swirled around the warmed space as it careened toward the Krai'kesh ship like dust being sucked up by a vacuum cleaner. Within moments the *Spirit of Zion* was no more. Not a piece of it remained in space. The giant gravity ship had consumed it whole, like some giant fish mentioned in ancient books.

Martin slumped in the captain's chair. How could they stand against such a weapon? An entire cruiser destroyed in minutes, shaken apart and sucked up, the crew having no chance to escape the gravitational field? No defense known to mankind could stand against that. "Give the order for the retreat. Communicate directly with the ships which are known Federation loyalists and order them to rendezvous at Pompero IV."

"Yes, sir, I am doing it now. When shall we shift?"

"Once all known loyalists and as many ground forces as possible are evacuated to our ship." If they survived that long surrounded by so many enemies. "Where is the *Dauntless*?"

"Sensors show she is still in the planet's atmosphere but is on the way out to space."

Hurry, Martin thought.

"HOLY SHIT," JOHN SAID. "Did you see that? An entire ship slurped up like a milkshake through a straw."

"I am more shocked at the destruction of the *Nightblade*," Ashley said. "Dawyn..."

John shook his head. "He's not dead. He can't be."

Ashley cleared her throat and changed the subject, clearly not wanting to discuss the chances of survival for the Supreme Commander. "The *Independence* is ordering all loyal Federation ships to evacuate to Pompero IV," Ashley said. "Zigana has asked that we come aboard the *Independence* before they depart."

"No," John said. "We have to find Emma. We're going our separate way."

"I don't think that's a good idea," Ashley said. "What if where Emma is being held is crawling with Krai'kesh? We are not invincible."

John slammed his fist down on the arm of his chair. "We can't just do nothing! We can't run further away while Emma slips away. This may be our only chance!"

Ashley put her hand on John's arm. "We will find her. But use your head, you big lug. We can't just go rushing in gun's blazing. We need support from the Federation military and right now the Federation military is pulling out of the system. We have to go with them."

Derek knew Ashley was right, but he sympathized with John. He felt like he was abandoning Selene in part by not going immediately after her. But he kept his silence. Selene was his girlfriend but Emma was their daughter. They would go wherever John and Ashley decided.

John sighed and hung his head. "You're right, Ash, as usual. The *Independence* it is."

Ashley did not make a smart remark at the mention of her usually being right. She merely squeezed his arm and smiled before returning to the console in front of her.

Ethan entered the cockpit at that moment. He sat down in the chair opposite Derek and said nothing.

"Hey, kiddo," John said. "All your boys settled in?"

"It's a little cramped, but they've been in tighter spots."

"I've been meaning to upgrade the *Dauntless*, you know," John said. "Just can't bring myself to scrap her."

Ethan snorted. "You always were a hoarder."

"Hey," John said in mock outrage. "I have an old soul. I don't like change. Which means I hold onto old stuff probably longer than I should."

"That's an understatement. You kept your gasoline car for like a hundred years after the full switchover to hover cars. Just kept it in your old garage with nowhere to drive it."

"Oh, and remember the pair of pants you owned for six decades," Ashley said. "I think there were like six layers of dust on them when you finally pulled them out."

"I'll have you know those were my skinny jeans," John protested. "They were a remnant from a dignified era."

"A dignified era that has come and gone four times since then."

"I think they're getting ready to make a comeback," Derek chimed in, feeling awkward participating in the family discussion. But he had seen people wearing synth-jeans which hugged their bodies awfully tight the last time he was on a more core-ward world.

"Ugh," Ethan said. "I think I had blocked those out in my memory. Thanks for dredging them up for me, Mom."

"Anything for my little boy," Ashley said, turning in her seat and blowing him a sarcastic kiss.

They seemed like a regular family. Almost. Derek didn't let the appearance fool him. He was sure Ethan hadn't given up his grudge against his family. He was also sure John and Ashley still felt hurt by his rejection. Perhaps considering Emma being captured, or worse, they felt they had to come together as a family. Derek smiled at the banter and would have relaxed if an entire fleet of traitorous ships and Krai'kesh invaders weren't clogging the space between them and the *Independence*. "I'm going to go take a turret," he announced.

"I'll take the other one," Ethan said. The dark blue of the upper atmosphere was rapidly morphing into the blackness of outer space. "It's been a while since I used one of those."

Derek took the top turret while Ethan took the bottom. He sighted his reticle and took a practice shot to calibrate himself. The turret needed no calibration but, like Ethan, it had been awhile since he fired a laser turret.

John plotted a straight path for the *Dauntless* to take to reach the *Independence*. Derek heard target lock warnings blare and then stop moments later repeatedly. "Is your targeting sensor on the fritz?" he asked through the comm.

"Nah, it's just so crazy out there we're being targeted by loyalists and traitors. No one is quite sure who to trust out there. It's our only saving grace or we'd have two dozen fighters and three dozen missiles barreling toward us right now."

Which we would be hard-pressed to survive, Derek thought. John had saved them once with an optical illusion before the Krai'kesh reached them that knocked him unconscious while Ashley had engaged in an equally dangerous feat of magic to manipulate a small asteroid field to their advantage, but they had been detected already and there were no asteroid fields nearby to call upon. What other tricks could they pull out of their sleeve if push came to shove?

Derek could not see the sensor outputs while in the turret seat but he could see what had to be the *Independence* in the distance. Her shields blurred as hit after hit struck them. He felt certain they would be unable to survive much longer.

John felt the same way, for he opened a channel to the *Independence*. "*Independence*, this is the *Dauntless*. We won't be able to reach you in time. We're going to activate our own shadow drive. Go ahead and jump."

"One moment." The line went silent for a moment. "The admiral agrees with your assessment and wishes you Godspeed in returning to Pompero IV."

"Thank the admiral for his well-wishes, but we don't need no stinking luck. *Dauntless* out." The link closed.

Derek rolled his eyes and imagined Ashley doing the same in the cockpit. Perhaps even Ethan was feeling embarrassed by his father? So they didn't need them in turrets after all. Derek did not hurry from the chair, instead watching the stars until the *Dauntless* passed through a void portal and the clear darkness of outer space was replaced with the cloudy darkness of shadow space.

Chapter 6 - Shadows of the Past

The surface of Coristair III neared as Rachel dove straight toward it. The wind whipped her hair back and made her already cold skin colder. A map in her mind's eye, projected by her implant, showed the landing area. She nudged herself in that direction and continued her rapid descent. When her implant warned her of impending impact she bound herself skyward and felt a tug on her back. The feeling moved to her head and shoulders as she became upright, her feet pointed toward the ground. Her descent almost halted. She laid off on the binding a little bit to pick up more speed but when she was twenty feet from the ground she increased the pull again and floated like a feather to the ground. *Too bad no one was around to see me nail such a great landing*, she thought.

Not that she was awed by such a landing. She had trained for years to perform such a maneuver and it came as second nature to her. She thought back to the first time she dove like that and broken both her legs upon landing. Damn that had hurt like a bitch for a few minutes.

She crouched down in case any observers had happened to see a single figure flying at high speed and unhooked her satchel from her back. She set it on the ground and withdrew her SX-1745 coilgun sniper rifle in a disassembled state. Muscle memory kicked in as she assembled the rifle for the umpteenth time. She surveyed her ammunition. Seven shells left. She only needed one.

She pulled up a map of the region she had downloaded before insertion with her implant. The compound containing her target lay twelve kilometers to the west. She walked in that direction, sniper rifle at the ready and dust crunching under her feet. She avoided shuffling her feet so as not to throw up dust and alert the sentries.

Her concerns were unfounded, however, for no sentries patrolled the area. Did they rely solely on long range sensors? Or had she not yet reached the perimeter? Ten minutes later she arrived at her destination. A cluster of ground cover on a hill overlooking a valley. Ten kilometers away sat the private villa of her target.

Rachel lay down in the ground cover and looked through the scope of her rifle. Her target, the dictator Dexter Ronin, sat on the portico of his private villa. His "wife," an indentured servant forced on penalty of death to serve him, sat across from him. He was speaking, his arms moving animatedly and his wife flashing an insincere smile.

The sniper rifle lay across the ground, couched against Rachel's shoulder. She made a few last-minute calculations, as the wind speed had picked up. A scene flashed in her mind of her first kill with the weapon. She pushed it aside, saving her lamentations for after the mission was accomplished.

A coilgun had been chosen for this job because of the occasional shimmer in front of Dexter. An energy shield surrounded his villa, stopping anything short of capitol ship turbo laser from breaching the perimeter. This job required more finesse, and a projectile weapon could fly straight through.

Her intel told her the villa was equipped with a complex system of sensors linked to an artillery battery. Upon detection of intruders on the perimeter or a weapon being discharged, the artillery battery would automatically target the point of origin within three seconds and fire.

They had not detected Rachel's movement yet, which suggested the sensors were calibrated to detect life signs rather than movement. That was all about to change. She would have to gun and run after confirming the kill.

Her finger went to the trigger. The dictator's head was in her sights. One shot, one kill, just like she'd been trained.

She fired. *One.*

The magnetically propelled projectile shot out faster than a chemically propelled bullet. Within an instant it impacted Dexter Ronin's head, blowing his brains out.

Two, she thought. Without further thought she accessed the power within and anchored herself to the space behind her. She flew straight backward, at a speed rivaling the bullet she'd just fired. She became upright as she flew, anchored to the hill behind her. From her perspective, the hill was down and she was falling backward toward it.

Three. The ground cover which had hidden her exploded as multiple artillery shells slammed down seconds after her departure. An ordinary assassin would have been turned to ash after such a strike.

She wasted no time binding herself space-ward. She flew toward the stratosphere at high speed, as if a vacuum was stuck to the top of head and dragging her up. "Any time now, guys," she said into her comm as she flew.

"Calculating intersection. You ready?"

"I was born ready."

As Rachel reached the stratosphere she bound herself to all directions. Her ascension halted but she did not fall or drift. She floated in one place. The *Renegade* flew up next to her. The side airlock opened. She bound herself to the inside of the ship and floated inside. Once inside she released her binding, the gravity of the planet below pulled her to the deck of the ship and her boots clomped loudly. The outer door closed and a hiss indicated air and pressure returning to the airlock. She removed her helmet and suit before it was complete and opened the inner door when the pressurization completed.

"Piece of cake," she said.

"I prefer pie, myself," Maggie said, seated at a bench in the common area of the *Renegade*. A bowl of synth-meal sat in front of her.

"Cake is a lie," said Reynaldo, sitting across from her with a drink in his hand.

"And you, Frank?" Rachel shouted toward the cockpit.

"Hey, I'm Swartheid. Leave me out of it."

"Even Swartheid picked a side during the war."

"Not right away. They waited to see who was winning to throw their hat in the ring."

"Sounds like us," Reynaldo said, taking a sip from his drink.

Rachel snorted. "You have it backwards. Any side we're on *is* the winning side."

"Whatever you say, boss," Maggie said, rolling her eyes, rising with a half-full bowl of stew and heading toward her quarters.

Rachel walked toward the refresher but stopped. She detected a gravitational shift behind her. She knew of only one thing that caused such.

Reynaldo spit out his drink and hurried to withdraw his pistol. "Boss, we got company." He pointed it toward the person behind Rachel.

Rachel sighed. "Put your weapon down, Reynaldo." She turned and confirmed the identity of their guest. "Hello, Aunt."

"Aunt?" Reynaldo spluttered. "She's your-your aunt? How the hell did she get aboard?"

Bridgette did not speak. She merely gave Reynaldo a cool glance before returning her gaze to Rachel. "We need to talk."

"Leave us," Rachel said.

"But, boss."

"I said, leave us," she said more firmly this time. "I need to speak with my aunt alone."

Reynaldo grumbled a "fine" and lumbered back to the table, grabbed his drink, and headed down the hall toward his quarters.

"I didn't think you would come back here after what happened last time," Rachel said after she heard a door slide shut down the hallway.

Bridgette remained where she was, assessing Rachel. "I was asked to come. And I wouldn't have been asked if it weren't important."

"I can guess who asked you. You can tell my father to go screw himself."

"This is bigger than you and your father. The Krai'kesh have returned."

"So what do you expect me to do about it? Just come running home?"

"The Federation needs you, Rachel."

"Hah. The same Federation that stood by and did nothing as my kind were oppressed and discriminated against? The Federation that let my mother die? No thanks."

"I can't change the past, or the facts. The Krai'kesh are using gravity as a weapon. You're the only one who stands a chance against that."

"No."

"Rachel..."

"I said no, Aunt Bridgette."

"I'm not leaving until..."

Rachel snapped. She bound Bridgette to the wall, forcing her to slam backward and stick there.

"You...agree...to...come," she finished.

"And I told you no. If you know what's good for you you'll leave and not return."

Bridgette shifted, leaving a shadowy mist behind.

Rachel's eyes widened. That hadn't happened the last time.

Bridgette rematerialized behind Rachel. "I went easy on you last time because, honestly, I didn't give a shit whether you came back to your father or not. I wasn't going to fight a brat for such a petty reason. But this...this is what I've been fighting for my *entire life*. I will do *anything* to see the Krai'kesh stopped once and for all."

"How did you do that?" was all Rachel could say. She knew for a fact Isabelle couldn't do that.

"There are many things you don't know about me," Bridgette said.

"Regardless, I'm not coming back with you."

"Then the Federation is doomed."

"Oh don't be so dramatic," Rachel scolded. "I'm sure Uncle Jason will discover some miracle technology to negate this weapon. Just give it time."

"We don't have time," Bridgette snapped. "Two planets have already been destroyed by this weapon and another left uninhabitable by another Krai'kesh weapon. We are losing and there's nothing we can do about it."

The Federation should have thought about that before they treated her so poorly. What did she owe them except her eternal ire? But perhaps she could help herself. "I'll come. On two conditions."

"Name them," Bridgette said instantly.

"One, my ship and my crew come with me."

"Fine," Bridgette said, looking around and sniffing.

Snobby bitch.

"Two, we get paid. A lot."

Bridgette gritted her teeth. "You're thinking about money at a time like this?"

"You expect us to win, right? Well, I expect to be paid enough that my crew and I never have to work again."

"How much?"

Rachel calculated numbers in her head. "A trillion Federation credits each."

"Fine," Bridgette bit out. "I'll see that it's done. Now are you ready to go? I wasn't lying about the urgency of this. Time is of the essence."

"Let me brief my crew first. Gotta get them on board."

"Two are in the corridor eavesdropping, as I'm sure the pilot was. I'm pretty sure they are already aware."

Ratted out, Reynaldo and Maggie emerged from around the corner. "How'd you know we were there?" Reynaldo asked.

"Two thousand years of staying one step ahead of the countless enemies who wanted me dead."

"Oh."

Rachel rolled her eyes. Apparently hubris ran on her father's side of the family. "Everyone okay with this?"

The door to the cockpit opened. "Just tell me where to fly, boss," Frank called.

"I'm in," Reynaldo said.

"Count me in," Maggie agreed. "I can buy a lot of shoes with a trillion credits."

"Forget shoes," Frank said. "I'll buy myself a ship ten times better than this hunk of..."

Rachel cleared her throat.

"...love. Hunk of burning love as it shoots through the sky."

"That's better," she said. "Let's get going," she said to Bridgette. But Bridgette was not listening. Her head was cocked to the side. She was communicating via her implant. Who would she be communicating with in the middle of nowhere near the outer edge of the Non-Aligned Planets?

Bridgette righted her head and blinked, re-focusing on Rachel. "We have to go, now."

"Okay," Rachel said, frowning. "We already agreed to go..."

"No, we really need to go. Your father's life is in danger."

"But..." her father was invincible. Or so she had always believed. Were the Krai'kesh truly that bad?

Bridgette didn't pay her any attention. She closed her eyes and Rachel felt their ship shift into shadow space. No void portal, no movement, just one moment and the next moment in shadow space.

Rachel made her way to the cockpit and sat in the co-pilot chair. The planet Rachel had just evacuated from took on a gray hue but disappeared a moment later, along with the entire solar system, as Bridgette moved the *Renegade* through shadow space without effort.

Unlike modern shifting, which used a shadow drive to artificially enter shadow space and move a ship at an accelerated but finite speed, Bridgette moved vast distances with what had to be a thought. Blink, a solar system with binary stars, blink, a single dwarf star. Blink, a sun with no planets in sight. Blink, blink, blink. The blinking continued, faster than Rachel could register, until they hovered amid a debris field.

An escape pod floated in the middle of the debris field.

"Activate the tractor beam," Rachel ordered before remembering she sat in the co-pilots chair and could activate it herself. She targeted the pod and triggered the beam. An overlay on the viewport showed where the beam was as it wrapped around the pod and pulled it toward the airlock.

"No need," Bridgette called.

Rachel turned around in her chair but Bridgette was gone. She stopped the tractor beam.

Moments later Bridgette rematerialized. She had someone else with her.

Rachel rose from her seat, unexpected butterflies flitting around in her stomach. What reason did she have to be nervous? She should be furious instead, readying her sidearm or preparing to punch him. Instead she exited the cockpit and studied her father.

His uniform was ripped and charred, his body seemed to have suffered burns that had yet to heal also. He raised his head. One of his eyes was swollen shut but the other seemed to look into her soul. "Rachel," her father said. "Is that really you?"

Rachel attempted to dislodge the lump in her throat by coughing. It didn't work. Instead she cleared her throat louder than she wanted. Reynaldo and Maggie were standing there looking back and forth she and her father. "It's me," was all she could get out.

He smiled at her despite a fat lip. "Come give your father a hug." He lifted his arms and grunted in pain.

"I don't want to hurt you," Rachel said. In reality, she didn't want to face her father. Yes, she was concerned for his safety but was she ready to embrace him again?

Her father frowned and lowered his arms. "I understand. Honestly, though, it looks worse than it is."

"In this instance, I think it is *worse* than it looks. It's likely you have internal bleeding and possibly organ damage," Bridgette said, crossing her arms.

"That would explain why the nanites aren't healing my outside appearance yet." He closed his eyes. "George agrees with your assessment. I see you learned a few things from your husband."

"Anyone who spends enough time with that man will pick up at least *something* useful," Bridgette replied. Her face softened. "You need to lie down and rest. Then you can tell us what happened."

Her father waved away Bridgette's concerns. "Bah, I don't need to sleep right now." He eyed one of the benches. "But I will have a seat."

Rachel brought him a glass of water. "Would you like something to eat?"

"Is it real food or synthetic?"

She gave him a wry smile. "What do you think?"

He took a large drink of water. "I think I need to eat something to keep up with the nanites. I guess gruel will have to do."

"Sorry we don't have the culinary capacity of the *Nightblade*."

He didn't say anything, just stared at a wall.

"Can you tell us what the hell happened?" Bridgette asked.

Her father shook his head to clear it and focused on Bridgette and then looked to Rachel. "We were betrayed."

"By who?" Bridgette asked.

"One of the commanders. He rammed his dreadnought into us, but not before giving some sort of veiled code. 'For the glory of Rae,' or something like that."

Bridgette's face went white. "You're sure those were his exact words?"

"Yes." He narrowed his eyes. "Why? What do you know?"

"The Cult of Rae have been around for centuries, in one form or another. Their names have changed but we always found a connection to that cult when we dug deeper."

"Did they advocate the return of the Krai'kesh? Because this cult seems to be in bed with the bastards."

Bridgette shook her head. "I never gave much credence to them. I figured it was another religious cult like the other few dozen that pop up all the time."

"Well, they're apparently ready to die for their cause and, if the fleet is any indication, they have sleepers hidden everywhere. Which I suppose goes with their cult being around for so many years."

"It isn't the first time we've dealt with insurrection," Bridgette said.

Rachel's father rolled his eyes. "No need to remind me. My wrists still hurt from those shackles fourteen hundred years later."

"My point is," Bridgette said, taking on a lecturing tone, "we've gotten through rebellion before and we'll do it again."

"In the past we haven't had the Krai'kesh breaking down the door as we cleaned house."

"I like a good challenge."

Rachel cleared her throat. "I hate to break up this family reunion," she didn't hate to do it, as the familiarity between her aunt and father reminded her of what she'd given up, "but what are we doing next?"

"Getting revenge," her father said, his gaze fierce as he met her eyes. "We make every single traitor to the Federation wish they'd never been born. And then we take the fight to the Krai'kesh and show them what they're really up against."

"We can start on Tar Ebon," Bridgette said.

"Tar Ebon?" Rachel asked. "Isn't that a bit," she waved a hand vaguely, "straightforward? Going right for the head instead of the lieutenants?"

"We have resources on Tar Ebon. The FIA headquarters is there, Fleet Command, the president."

"We can't trust Fleet Command," Dawyn said. "Not after the insurrection I saw among the admiralty. It is rampant."

"Well, I can guarantee there are no traitors in FIA headquarters waiting to betray me."

"Fine, set course for Tar Ebon, Frank." She looked between Dawyn and Bridgette. "I hope you're right about this. We just painted the *Renegade* - I don't want it scratched."

Chapter 7 - Abandon Hope

The door to the bridge of the *Goldstar* slid open and Selene, Emma, and the remaining four pilots of Victory Squadron were led, in stun-cuffs, inside. Emma also wore a collar around her neck to suppress her magic. Selene's brother, Frederick, stood with his hands clasped behind his back as in the distance more Krai'kesh vessels appeared, firing at unseen targets she knew were the surviving House Vivendi employees she'd assured would be given safe passage out of the system. Men, women, children, all trusting her. All dead or dying.

Frederick turned to her and smiled. "Ah, there's my little sister."

Selene spat on the floor to show just how much his false familiarity mattered to her. "You gave me your word," she said point blank.

His frown faded a little before he renewed it and smiled even more. "Come on, you can't be mad at me. It's just business. You know how it goes."

"Monster."

"You don't mean that," Frederick said. "Take it back." He had always been sensitive to the opinions of others. He desired to be liked by everyone.

"You're a despicable, detestable, deplorable monster with no compassion and I am horrified we're related."

"You shouldn't have said that, little sister." He snapped his fingers and Emma and Selene were dragged to the side by the guards. The other four pilots remained where they were.

Frederick drew his pistol, a gold-plated coilgun, and came to stand a couple of meters in front of the four pilots. He raised his pistol. "This is the punishment for your disrespect."

"No!" Selene shouted.

Frederick pulled the trigger. The bullet exploded through the head of the first pilot, blood splattering everywhere. He did not pause and shot the second pilot, then the third. He looked at Selene as he aimed at the fourth pilot. "You did this, sister." He pulled the trigger and the fourth pilot died. Blood and brain matter seeped out onto the deck of the bridge. "Clean this up," he snapped and a guard exited the bridge, presumably to get the cleaning crew. "What a pity," he said, no remorse in his voice.

Selene glared at him, wishing she could shoot lasers from her eyes. She clenched her fists. "Am I going to be next?"

Frederick's eyes widened in surprise. "No! Of course not. You're family, I wouldn't hurt family."

I would, Selene thought. *I will kill you given the chance.* Would she really, though? She thought back to her youth when she and her brother would play together during the carefree days before he went off to mentor with Father. That changed him. He went from a caring, if vain, young boy to a cold-hearted ruthless man. "For now," was what she said.

Frederick didn't seem to hear her comment. "Ah, our guest of honor has arrived. Let us go down to the docking bay and greet him."

Guest of honor? Who is he talking about?

The guards ushered them down to the docking bay, Frederick leading the way. Fighters were nowhere to be seen. Instead an organic-looking vessel sat there. No docking clamps touched it. The Krai'kesh were aboard the ship. A hole opened in the side of the ship, like an airlock but with no visible doorway before it spiraled open. The same material that covered the ship flowed down to form a ramp. A tall bi-pedal Krai'kesh, larger than the commanders she'd seen before, exited the ship. Four tentacle-like appendages waved from the rear of its head. It carried a staff and used it like a walking stick. Behind it followed four of the smaller commanders Selene was accustomed to seeing. The large Krai'kesh stopped in front of Frederick.

"Honored Overseer Harkesh, welcome to the *Goldstar*." He bowed and extended a hand.

"Is this the Eternal?" he asked in fluent Common. He raised a hand and pointed a claw at Emma, ignoring Frederick's word and hand.

Frederick cleared his throat, a sign Selene knew meant he was either nervous or annoyed. She hoped he was annoyed and showed it so the Krai'kesh overseer would skewer him with his staff. "Yes, Overseer. Our trap worked just as you said it would. They suspected nothing."

"She is punier than I expected," the overseer said. He grabbed Emma's face with a claw. She grit her teeth and glared at him but did not speak. "It will not be a challenge to break her."

"I'll never break," Emma declared. "Do your worst."

The overseer laughed, a horrifying evil laugh. "Perhaps I was mistaken. She has a fire in her. But all fires must go out eventually, when starved enough for fuel or air. I think I shall enjoy breaking her." His gaze swept to Selene. She felt terror as their eyes met. An evil seemed to emanate from the overseer and it sent a chill up her spine. "And this one? Is she an Eternal also?"

"No, honored Overseer, she is of no consequence."

The overseer turned back to Frederick. "I will be the judge of who is of consequence or not. She is alive and standing before me for a reason. Explain or I will cut her down."

Selene swallowed hard.

"She is my sister," Frederick said quickly. Why was he so reluctant to reveal their family ties?

"You hold your own sister captive?" the overseer asked, his tone neutral.

"She...betrayed our house. She is being punished for her indiscretion and actions against House Artois."

The overseer turned back to Selene and lifted his staff. He thrust it up beneath Selene's chin. She could feel the sharp tip of it almost breaking the skin. "My people execute traitors."

"Of course, sir, but we are trying to rehabilitate her. To change her mind and return her to the fold."

"A waste of time," the overseer said, but he lowered his staff. "But she is no concern to me. I will take the Eternal." He barked something in his own language and two commanders stepped forward. They each took one of Emma's arms and lifted her up.

"Of course, my lord," Frederick bowed again. "My life for Rae."

"The god-emperor is pleased," Overseer Harkesh said. "Continue to please him and his favor will be upon you. Fail him and you will wish for death."

"I understand, my lord," Frederick said, his voice shaky and sounding uncertain. How committed was he, really?

Selene locked eyes with Emma. Emma gave her an infinitesimal nod, as if to say everything would be fine. She claimed she would resist the efforts of the overseer to break her, but was that bravado? Or would she truly resist? *I will rescue you*, she thought, despite her implant being blocked from accessing the network aboard the *Goldstar*.

Overseer Harkesh turned and stalked back to his ship and ascended the ramp. The other four commanders followed, two dragging Emma along as she kicked and squirmed. The ramp retracted when all were aboard and the side of the ship closed back up. It rose from the deck, turning and left.

Frederick shivered. "He gives me the creeps."

"Why did you get into bed with the Krai'kesh, Frederick? What did they offer you?"

Frederick blinked. "Why, eternal life. The god-emperor showed us his power and told us of His coming. He said to follow him or perish. Father, being a smart man, decided to side with the Krai'kesh."

"The Krai'kesh have only been in our galaxy for a few weeks," Selene said, confused.

He made a tutting noise. "Oh, dear sister, how naive you are. The Krai'kesh have been in our galaxy for more years than you know." He smiled like he used to when he knew something she didn't.

That was the first she had heard of such a thing. "How long?"

Frederick shrugged. "Long enough to plant followers and agents throughout the galaxy. Even now a Federation-wide coup is being executed by people from all walks of life. Finally a use for the poor. The Federation is dead, it just doesn't know it yet."

"You really think the Krai'kesh will give *you*, a traitor, eternal life? Don't you see they're just using you?" She waved her hands around for emphasis. "They're trying to divide us," she made a chopping motion, "so they have an easier time exterminating us."

"Save your breath, sister. I will not hear more lies from you." He paused to make sure she wouldn't continue speaking. "Now, I have accommodations prepared for you so you may rest in comfort."

Selene laughed. "Rest in comfort? As a prisoner?"

"You will be restricted in your movements outside of your room for your own safety. We wouldn't want you to hurt yourself or anyone else of course." He turned to exit the docking bay. The guards prodded Selene to follow.

Like you, she thought. "So a gilded cage."

"If you would prefer a... less accommodating room that can certainly be arranged."

She thought perhaps she should take an ordinary prison cell as a way of protesting the capture of Emma and as a symbol of solidarity. But no, she needed to keep her strength up if she was to escape when the time was right. Only by playing along and remaining some place where she could get plenty of food, water, and rest could she hope to do so. She took a deep breath. Time to eat crow. "No, you're correct, brother. I am grateful for the room you have prepared for me. Please forgive me for my outburst."

Her submissive comment seemed to satisfy her brother, for his dangerous frown morphed into a large smile. He clapped. "Excellent!" He looked to the guards. "Please show my sister to her quarters." He waved at the stun-cuffs. "And get rid of those abysmal things. She has nowhere to run."

Be careful cornering a caged animal, Selene thought. "Where are you going next?" she asked.

"Home. Our mission here is complete and Father wishes to stay out of things for a bit longer before we directly intervene in the war. He will be...surprised...to see you."

Surprised was an understatement. She would be lucky to leave his presence alive.

The guards escorted her to her "quarters," removed her stun-cuffs, and shoved her inside. A lavish cabin with a canopy bed, full sani-room with a hot tub, and gilded mirror met her. The click of a lock being engaged broke the illusion that she was on a luxury cruise liner. She pulled back a pair of drapes, revealing a large rectangular duraglass viewport. Outside she could see House Artois ships congregating near the *Goldstar* and Krai'kesh ships beyond. She shut the shades in disgust and flopped down on the canopy bed.

Her thoughts drifted to Derek and the rest of the fleet. Her brother had mentioned betrayal - had the fleet been ambushed like her squadron had? If so, were they even still alive? She couldn't imagine the *Independence* being destroyed, but judging by how many Krai'kesh vessels were in one system it seemed likely they could overpower the *Independence* if she were beset with traitors and Krai'kesh ships.

Home, she thought. How would she face her father? Was her brother right - did he want her dead? What about her mother? Would she fall in line with her father in disowning her or would she embrace her long-lost daughter? She had a week until she found out.

SELENE ENTERED THE dining chamber, feeling uncomfortable in the dress her brother insisted she wear. It still smelled of plastic from being manufactured by nanites. *They need to clean their nozzles*, she thought. Her tutor in school had stressed that when they discussed nanite engineering. He said "Nanite manufacturing is only as good as the raw materials. If you have poor components no number of nanites and no amount of processing time can make a good product. Nanites speed up the manufacturing process drastically but they can still suffer from the same flaws of older processes." That was one of the few lectures she remembered on that topic - she'd daydreamed during most of the others.

His brother's face lit up when he saw her, partially because he was happy to see her but also because the light reflected off his face due to how much make-up he was wearing. When had her brother become so effeminate? He stood and extended his arms out in front of him. "You look marvelous, little sister."

Selene rolled her eyes and tugged at the portion of her dress that draped her legs. Must he always remind her she was his younger sister? And what compelled him to think she liked dresses. "You know I don't like dresses." In fact, she had worn dresses as a girl only under extreme duress, preferring to wear trousers or shorts, much to her mother's chagrin.

Her words did not seem to faze him. "Please, sit, I've had your favorite dish prepared." He ushered and servants emerged from a hidden door carrying trays of food. They set three trays in front of Selene and opened them one-by-one. Inside the first was a roast beef, sliced. The second tray contained a bowl with macaroni and cheese, while the third contained a strawberry hash she used to love.

Despite her hatred for her brother, and her situation, she felt a moment of joy seeing the food she loved as a child placed before her. "This must have cost a fortune," she said. "The beef, the strawberries."

Her brother waved away her observation. "Only the best for the flagship of House Artois. We've improved our supply chain since you left, sister. Beef supply has been up five percent and strawberry production up three percent year-over-year for ten years. Business is booming."

Selene felt the urge to talk shop - to ask her brother about the business, the finances, how things were going. After all, that was what they discussed when they were children and later teenagers - it had all been about the business. But she stopped herself. *Don't succumb to Stockholm Syndrome*, she thought. She didn't know where Stockholm was or the origin of the phrase, but she knew what it meant; if she weren't careful she would fall into the trap of sympathizing with her captors and perhaps even wanting to remain there. The thought horrified her, so instead she took a bite of pasta smothered in cheese, chewed and said, "Business built on the backs of the working poor." A true statement, though one overlooked for most of her life. She had been blind.

Her brother chewed his bite of beef casually. He waved his fork around. "We give the people jobs, my dear. Without us the 'working poor,' as you put it, would have nothing and would starve."

"No, without the corporations and merchants the people would keep more of their possessions and be able to rise to something better than themselves." It was an argument she'd heard rarely while in the Commerce Sector - such thoughts considered sedition and resulted in prison or execution - but was common in the Federation, which was built on a free market economy. She had been surprised that ordinary people could rise to any position they worked hard enough to achieve in the Federation.

"Such a naive viewpoint," her brother said in a condescending tone. "How is the food?" he asked, changing the subject.

"Just like home," she admitted.

Her brother clapped. "I knew you would like it!" He turned to one of the servants. "Give my sister's compliments to the chef." The servant bowed and exited the room. "Now come, sister, tell me what you have been doing for all these years. Surely you haven't been flying a dirty starfighter at the edge of the galaxy the entire time."

It's not dirty, Selene thought, but then remembered the layer of dust she had wiped off the seat adjustment bar just the other day. Okay, maybe it was dirty, but she considered it well worn. "What do you care?" she asked.

He affected a hurt look. "You wound me, dear sister. Father may have exiled you."

"Disowned me, you mean."

"Yes, yes. But I still thought of you from time-to-time."

Selene snorted. She doubted his statement. How could she trust any word from her brother after the way he betrayed her trust by executing the employees of House Vivendi and her fellow pilots? Not to mention giving Emma to the Krai'kesh. But she decided to indulge him. "I enlisted right away in the Federation Navy. I served my time and *chose* to fly a dusty fighter at the edge of nowhere."

Frederick sniffed her statement. "What a dreadful experience. I am sorry you had to endure such crass conditions."

"I *chose* to endure them. And they were still better than the conditions most of *your* employees live in."

He ignored her accusation and took a sip from his wine glass. "Well, we will soon be back in civilization, my dear sister, and all will be well again. You'll see just what you were missing during your...sabbatical."

Selene chose to ignore his comment this time. "So you took over House Vivendi. How many more houses do you plan to take over?"

"Well, we're still finishing up the integration and consolidation efforts, during which time we'll remove redundancies."

"You mean kill those employees who are no longer useful."

He frowned. "We do not kill them. We lay them off."

"Same difference. When they can't support their family and starve you've as good as killed them."

Her brother waved his hand. "I cannot be expected to care about the welfare of all my employees, sister. I make decisions that are best for the house, not out of misplaced emotion."

"Misplaced emotion? You mean things like compassion and empathy. Yes, those are so very misplaced. Heaven forbid a corporation or merchant house *care* about the welfare of their employees."

"We care about our employees. But once they cease to become our employees we no longer have the manpower to continue caring for every one of them."

Selene shook her head. Arguing with him and over a decade of indoctrination at the hands of their father was going to get her nowhere. She wiped her mouth with a napkin and stood. "Thank you for dinner, brother, but I wish to retire to my rooms now." *My prison cell*, she thought. Three nights in her room had yielded poor sleep, low energy, and left her to dwell on her situation for hours on end.

"Leaving so soon?" he asked in a tone that bordered on a whine.

"Yes." Selene did not stop as she left the dining room. Her guards fell in behind her and followed her back to her room. She entered and waited for the click of the lock before stripping off her itchy, smelly dress and changing into something more comfortable. Within ten minutes she was asleep, dreaming of being anywhere but there.

Chapter 8 - Betrayal

A void portal opened in the space above the planet Pompero IV. The *Independence* emerged first, followed by the remnants of their fleet and the Black Fleet.

"Any hostile contacts?" Martin asked.

"Negative, sir. No target lock warnings or signs of Krai'kesh."

"Defense forces?"

"The sector fleet is in high orbit around Pompero IV, sir. They are moving toward us and launching fighters."

Standard procedure, Martin thought. "Admiral Grace Bellanca, yes?"

"Correct, sir."

"She was one of the supporters of us during the vote the admirals took trying to depose the Supreme Commander," Martin mused.

"Then it is likely she can be trusted, sir."

"Let's hope so. Keep an eye on them, though. Prepare to raise the shields at any sign of betrayal from them. How many of our ships survived?"

Zigana adopted a grim expression. "One cruiser, two dreadnoughts, three destroyers, four frigates, and five corvettes."

"So few. How many defectors?"

"It was difficult to tell, sir. Many ships were lost during the cross-fire or when the Krai'kesh emerged, so it is difficult to count how many traitor ships are still remaining."

"I feel like a damn fool. As soon as that commander told us only Victory Squadron had been destroyed I should have been more suspicious. I just didn't expect this." He should have. History showed that rebellions, coups, and insurrections had occurred throughout the Federation's history. It was not a new phenomenon. There were always parties ready to seize power for themselves and willing to die, and kill, for their goals. "Put me through to Admiral Bellanca please." He took a deep breath, preparing to deliver the news he never thought he would be required to.

The image of Admiral Bellanca appeared on the holo-display. "Admiral Rigsby, this is a surprise." She furrowed her brows. "Where is the rest of the fleet? Did you split up?"

Martin grimaced. "Admiral Bellanca, it is an honor to speak with you, but alas I come with grave tidings." He cleared his throat. "A few hours ago the Black Fleet and my own fleet were betrayed. Rogue elements within the Federation Navy engaged in coordinated strikes and sabotage attempts across the fleet. Several ships turned on us, while uprisings on other ships were put down. To make matters worse, the Krai'kesh also arrived and started attacking loyalist ships."

"I notice the *Nightblade* is not among your ships..." the admiral trailed off.

Martin swallowed hard and closed his eyes for a moment before re-opening them. "I regret to inform you the *Nightblade* was destroyed because of the first betrayal by said rogue elements. An explosive was set off inside the docking bay and then it was rammed by a dreadnought."

"And the Supreme Commander?" she asked.

"We were not able to locate his body or confirm his death, but we also were not able to rescue him. We were forced to retreat before search & rescue operations could conclude." *Or even commence.*

"So the Supreme Commander could be in enemy custody? Or dead?" She sounded shaken up. Is that how he sounded?

"I'm afraid so, Admiral."

She blinked rapidly. Was she crying? "Well then, we must press on. What is the next step?"

Martin hadn't thought that far ahead. Their retreat to the Pompero system had not been planned.

A beep sounded, followed by an icon appearing on the sensor display behind the image of Admiral Bellanca. "One moment please, Admiral." He turned to Zigana. "Who is that?"

"The *Dauntless*, sir."

"Good. Ask them to come aboard, please." At least the Eternals aboard that ship had survived. To lose three Eternals in one day would possibly be a bigger morale hit than even he could sustain. He shook his head. No, Dawyn was *not* dead, not definitively, not confirmed. He was resourceful. Surely he would have had contingency plans in place, right? He looked back at the admiral. "For now we are going to perform repairs and retrofit the remnants of our fleet. Then I'm going to contact Fleet Command and the president and inform them of the situation. We do not yet know if this is a widespread rebellion or whether it was localized to this one spot. We will have to proceed cautiously and use care deciding who to tell."

"Of course, Martin. You have the full support of my fleet, but I am hesitant to leave my sector undefended for too long."

"I understand, Admiral, but that seems to be what the Krai'kesh want us to do. Sit in one spot while they pick off our planets, and destroy them, one-by-one."

"The alternative is to spread ourselves too thin, isn't it?"

"Yes," Martin acknowledged. "I am going to recommend to the president that we begin evacuation of the surrounding sectors core-ward and focus our military assets on the more highly populated systems." *I'm condemning millions of people to die*, he thought. Not all the people would be able to evacuate and so there *would* be casualties - lots of them. But in this case the good of the many outweighed the good of the few.

"That will be a massive evacuation effort. Existing worlds could rebel against taking on so many refugees."

"I will leave that to the politicians. My job is to protect human lives and that is what I'm going to do, politics be damned."

"My fleet will, of course, render whatever aid we can."

"That is greatly appreciated, Grace."

The link closed. "They're recalling their fighters, sir, and moving back into orbit."

"Good. Open a connection to Fleet Command."

"Yes, sir." Moments later the Fleet Command logo displayed on the holo-display, followed by the image of a colonel. "Fleet Command, how may I direct your inquiry?"

"I need to speak to Admiral Hensen. This is Admiral Martin Rigsby." The Chief of Naval Operations was his first stop before moving on to the president and senate.

"One moment, please." The colonel sounded bored. The image muted for a few moments before returning. "I'm sorry, sir, Admiral Hensen is indisposed right now."

Martin grit his teeth. "Tell Admiral Hensen it is about the *Nightblade* and the Supreme Commander. Now."

"Yes, sir. One moment." The image muted again. A moment stretched into a few minutes before the colonel returned. "I'm patching you through to the admiral now, sir."

"Thank you," Martin said, though he wanted to tell the man off. To be fair, it wasn't his fault - he had relayed what the admiral told him to say.

Admiral Hensen appeared on the display seconds later. His bald head reflected the ceiling light. "Admiral Rigsby, my assistant tells me you have urgent news about the *Nightblade* and the Supreme Commander? I certainly hope this is important."

"It is, admiral. I regret to inform you that the *Nightblade* has been destroyed. The Supreme Commander is MIA."

Admiral Hensen blinked but remained silent. At last he spoke in an uncertain voice. "Destroyed? MIA? Admiral Bordekov was right."

An icy chill ran up Martin's back. "Admiral Bordekov?"

"Yes, she contacted me and told me the Supreme Commander was dead. I didn't believe her, of course, but now... What happened?"

"The Supreme Commander is missing in action, sir, not confirmed dead. But what occurred was that rogue elements within the Navy betrayed us. They were supported by the Krai'kesh."

"I see," he said. That wasn't the reaction Martin had expected. "This is disturbing." He didn't sound disturbed to Martin. "We must notify the other Joint Chiefs at once and call a meeting. A new supreme Commander must be selected."

"With respect, sir, the Supreme Commander is not confirmed dead. We cannot select a new one."

"An interim Supreme Commander is what I meant," Admiral Hensen amended.

A little soon to be replacing Dawyn, Martin thought. "I understand, sir."

"I will be in touch. Where are you located?"

Something inside Martin compelled him to lie. "Deltar II, sir. We're badly damaged and affecting repairs before moving on." Out of the corner of his eye he saw Zigana jerk his head up.

"Good. Maintain your position while I arrange the meeting with the Joint Chiefs and the admiralty." He paused. "Thank you for your service, Admiral."

Martin nodded. "Of course, sir." He waited until the link closed before looking at Zigana. "Send a probe to Deltar II."

"Sir?"

"Just do it, Zigana. I have a theory but I want to test it out first."

"Yes, sir. Would you like me to connect you with the president now?"

"Not yet. I suspect I will have one chance to contact him and I don't want to tip my hand."

Zigana gave him a puzzled look but nodded.

"Will you ask Captain Edgerton to come to the bridge, please?"

"Of course, sir"

Martin occupied the next several minutes reviewing repair and re-supply reports and signing off on requisition forms. He reviewed the after-action casualty reports. Too many men and women lost. For being a carrier they had lost most of their complement of fighters. They were like a shark with too many of its teeth shattered. He prayed they would be able to acquire more before long. But even more pressing than fighters was the need for pilots. All the fighters in the galaxy would be useless without trained pilots to fly them.

At last the door to the bridge slid open and Captain Edgerton, his wife, son, and Lieutenant Jamison entered.

"Heya, your admiralness," John said.

Martin sighed. "Captain Edgerton. I would have thought you would be more...morose...given the circumstances."

"Oh, about Emma?"

"And the Supreme Commander."

"I was, and still would be, if I thought they were dead. But I know Emma and Dawyn are both alive, so, no sadness, man."

"How can you be so certain?" Sure, Martin *hoped* Dawyn remained alive, but he had no proof.

"Well, the same commander who said Emma was dead also rammed his ass into the *Nightblade* and committed suicide so he's not exactly a reliable witness. As for Dawyn, he's been declared dead more times than I can count. There was this one time a mountain fell on him..."

"That was you, dear," Ashley interjected.

"...oh yeah, on me. Another time he drowned, another time he was flayed, another time..."

Martin held up a hand. "Okay, I get it. He is resilient. But can he survive in the vacuum of space?"

"If he's unprotected, no, but my guess is he had some trick up his sleeve. That man always has a contingency plan."

"Well, let us hope he comes back to us soon. I'm afraid the rogue elements have already begun to pounce." He left unsaid the full details of his suspicions.

"No doubt," Ashley said.

"What did you want to speak to us about, Admiral?" Ethan Edgerton asked.

"I need someone to perform a reconnaissance mission to the system where Emma and the other pilots of Victory Squadron were last seen. We need to find out the full extent of what happened there and whether they are still alive. Can you do that?"

"That aligns with what we were already planning to do," Ashley said. "Bringing our daughter home is our top priority now."

"And it is a mission I would not hesitate to stand in the way of." Not that he thought he could contain them against their will if they had their mind set on finding her.

"What else did you want us up here for, chief?" John asked.

Martin looked around at the bridge crew members. He didn't suspect any of them exactly, but after what happened, he couldn't be too careful. "Join me in my quarters, please." He led them out of the bridge and through the corridors to his quarters. Once inside he shut the door. His quarters were regularly swept for listening devices, so he had a reasonable expectation they would not be overheard.

"What's with all the cloak and dagger?" John asked.

Martin surveyed the four in front of him. "Perhaps I am being paranoid, but with the number of defections to the enemy side I no longer know who I can trust."

"Even your own bridge crew?"

"Yes, even them. I fear there could be a second wave of sleeper agents waiting to strike until a second signal comes through or something of the sort. Call me paranoid if you will, but I cannot afford to be caught unaware again."

John adopted a thoughtful expression. "I mean, that's good and all, but you can't just push everyone away either, Admiral. Doing that will hurt morale among your fleet and possibly make the crew lose confidence in you. Believe me, we've been through this before and I know what it's like. Ash and I had to hide for one hundred years, never knowing who we could truly trust. We had some close calls and we went through some years where we didn't trust anyone and lived like hermits early on. But in the end we realized we had to be reasonable and let *some* people in."

"I suppose you're right. But while you're here, I need to warn you about certain individuals within the fleet that I believe may be part of this revolution. The first is one Admiral Bordekov. She claimed at the time she resigned her command but I believe now that may have been a sham, or that the trap which caught the *Nightblade* in its trap was orchestrated in response to the failed attempt by dissidents to oust Dawyn as the Supreme Commander. But it gets worse. When I discussed the defectors with the Joint Chief representing the Navy he did not seem as concerned as I expected and spoke of finding a replacement for the Supreme Commander position. I found that odd."

"That is odd," Ashley said. "So you think things could have escalated all the way to the high command?"

"It's possible. The Joint Chiefs are appointed by the senate, not by the Supreme Commander. We don't know how deep this conspiracy goes."

"Do you suspect the president?" Ethan asked.

Martin shook his head. "By all accounts he was attacked by the Krai'kesh. I doubt they would do that if they saw him as an ally. I will be contacting him soon, once I have more proof."

"How are you going to get more proof?" John asked.

"I told the Joint Chief of the Navy a different system that we were recovering in. I sent a probe to watch the system. If the Krai'kesh, pirates, or any other parties show up there I will have evidence to support that he was the leak, since he was the only one I told."

"Clever," Ashley said. "But that will tip your hand, won't it?"

Martin sighed. "Yes, and I will have to act fast at that point to present my evidence to the president and hope that he can do something to stop the insurgents before they topple the government."

"I'll reach out to some contacts I have in the Shadow Watch Guards," Ethan said. "I'll ask them to tighten security around the president and keep a closer eye on things."

"And I'll ask Bridgette to put the FIA on a higher alert for domestic terrorist actions," Ashley said.

"If you can find her. She's a bit flighty," John said.

"That's your sister-in-law you're talking about and she isn't flighty. She has the entire Federation to protect from threats just like these insurgents."

"I must have mixed her up with your brother." He chuckled.

Ashley cracked a smile. "I'll give you that one, though I think *he* would argue he's just distracted and on the verge of one breakthrough or another."

"Do you think we can count on your brother to develop new weaponry to help fight the Krai'kesh?" Martin asked.

Ashley pursed her lips. "He's been out of the defense industry for centuries, preferring instead to study implants, genetics, quantum physics, and fields I can't even remember. But that doesn't mean he won't come back to building weapons and defensive technologies if we ask him. In fact, I imagine Bridgette or Dawyn already has."

"Well if you speak with him, tell him the gravity weapons used by the Krai'kesh are the biggest threat we face in this war. Any solution he has that can nullify their ability to use such weapons would be greatly appreciated."

"I'll tell him next time I talk to him."

"We should go, Admiral," John said. "We'll be in touch about what we find, but if Emma isn't there we aren't coming back here. We're going to follow the trail until we find her."

Martin nodded, though a selfish part of him worried what would happen if another gravity ship threatened to destroy a planet and the Eternals weren't there. "I completely understand, Captain Edgerton. Do what you need to do. However, depending on how this coup shakes out I may need you on Tar Ebon sooner rather than later."

"Just remember to not see enemies in every shadow, Admiral. It will help you keep your sanity," Ashley said.

Martin bowed his head. "I will bear that in mind, Mrs. Edgerton."

THREE HOURS AFTER THE *Dauntless* departed to find out the fate of Victory Squadron, Martin lay in bed next to his wife when a beep awoke him. "Yes, Zigana," he said.

"I apologize for disturbing you, sir," Zigana said. "But I thought you should know the probe picked up activity."

"Don't tell me. The Krai'kesh."

"Correct, sir, along with two rogue Federation ships. They appeared, probed the area, and then departed."

"All right, I'll be to the bridge shortly to call the president. I need to get dressed first."

"Of course, sir."

Chapter 9 - Bloodbath

"Whee, nice quarters, m'lady," Corbin said. He went over to the minibar and picked up a decanter of alcohol and sniffed it. "Whew, makes me eyes water."

"No drinking on the job," Kimberly said as she laced up her boots. She was glad to be rid of the high heels that formed part of her cover.

"It's part of me cover," he said, taking a drink. "The drunk imbecilic servant tha' everyone will underestimate." He winked at her.

"I think you're taking your cover a little too seriously." She stood up and donned a brown leather jacket she had picked up at a high-end clothing store. She would shine outdoors thanks to the diamonds sewn into the sleeves. The salesperson assured her the jacket was hand-sewn, a rarity anywhere in the civilized parts of the galaxy.

"If oi don't, lass, someone will become suspicious. Ye should do the same." He took another drink.

"Would it be in character for me to take that decanter and break it over your head?" The last thing she needed was him drunk when they met the resistance forces.

He shrugged. "If oi did something real bad ta offend yeh."

Kimberly stepped toward him.

His eyes went wide and he hugged the decanter close. "Oh no ye don't."

Kimberly smiled and stopped. "Just keeping you on your toes." She adopted a somber expression and looked at Baillidh. "Any bugs here?"

Baillidh shook his head. He wore black trousers and a tight-fitting synth shirt. A brimmed hat would shield his eyes from the sun. "No, ma'am. Nor did I expect there to be any. The Federation has no reason to be suspicious of our identities. They believe you are a wealthy merchant, nothing further."

"Was there any surveillance equipment focused on us during the ride to the embassy?"

"Nothing aimed at capturing our audio or other communications while inside."

"Good. It means no one suspects us yet. Come on, Corbin, you drunk. We need to meet the resistance operatives."

"'Ey, oi'm not drunk yet. Give me five minutes to get inta character." He took another drink.

On their way out of the embassy the ambassador spotted them. He sauntered over, brazenly looking Kimberly up and down, even though she wore more functional clothing than upon their arrival.

"Ah, Miss Sommrich," he said. "Just the person I was looking for!"

You mean the person you were looking at, Kimberly thought, but forced a smile. "Ambassador Barrius, what can I do for you?"

"I want to invite you to a gala tonight at the estate of House Artois. Would you do me the honor of accompanying me?"

Kimberly kept her expression neutral. Why was he inviting *her* of all people? She paused for a moment, as if checking her schedule in her mind. At last she smiled and looked him in the eyes. "Why, I would be delighted to accompany you, Ambassador."

"Excellent, I shall see you there. It begins at eight this evening."

He's not even going to pick me up?

She nodded her head slightly. "I shall be there."

HALF AN HOUR LATER the three FIA agents waited at the gates leading to the Dark Zone, an area populated by the working poor Corbin talked about. They rode in a hover car which they rented for the price of a new car on most Federation worlds. In fact, Kimberly had almost balked at the price before Corbin reminded her she was supposed to be a wealthy business woman. Wealthy business women would not balk at any price. Feeling chastised and exploited, she had forced a smile as she handed over her cred-chip. She had to admit the seats were plusher than seats in the much less expensive rentals on other worlds. Comfort came at a cost, and it wasn't on her dime anyway.

The guards at the gate leading through the massive border wall gave them a curious look as he checked their credentials. "Why is a person of your standing going out *there*?" A derisive sneer suggested what he thought of the Dark Zone.

Kimberly was about to launch into an explanation about the fake business dealings she was going to engage in with factory owners and whatnot but decided that was out of character and instead said, "That is none of your concern. My business is my own. You would do well to remember that."

For several heartbeats she feared the guard would become angry and bar them from leaving. Instead he bowed and handed back their documents. "Forgive me, m'lady, I meant no offense. Please proceed."

Hiding a bewildered expression, she spoke to Corbin. "Drive, servant."

"Yes, ma'am," Corbin said, slurring his words but driving slowly through the security checkpoint. Was it an act or was he truly drunk??

Beyond the gates smog filled the air and veiled the clouds above, a sharp contrast to the blue sky and sunshine back on the other side. The air scrubbers truly made a difference.

Their hover-car traveled down a road rank with potholes as they made their way toward the town of Vortville, making Kimberly thankful to be floating above them.

"Ugh, those fumes are horrible," Kimberly said.

"Aye, the smell o' sulfur and fossil fuels bein' burnt."

"They're still using such archaic energy sources?" Kimberly asked.

"The common folk do, yes. The rich folk have nuclear power plants or shadow generators powering their cities. If the poor folk want power they have ta work in the power plants to generate it."

"The corporations could easily afford to bring in greater sources of power and wipe these ancient power plants out. Why don't they?"

"They have no reason to, lass. If they take away a labor source, a job-creator, unemployment rises. When unemployment rises people get unhappy. When people get unhappy they start ta question the status quo. When that happens revolution and resistance soon follow. And considerin' ninety percent o' the populace are common folk, that would be bad news for the bourgeois on this planet."

"They could use a good revolution," Kimberly said, watching a group of grungy children run down the street as they passed. "Or the Federation could liberate them."

Corbin let out a belly laugh. "Oh, lass, the Federation don't care about the Commerce Sector."

"What do you mean?" she asked.

"Ta start, they've got their hands full with the Krai'kesh and probably the Empire by now. Second, even if the war were over and we won there's still the fact tha' the feudal system here is so ancient and ingrained in the society of their culture tha' people would not *want* ta be liberated. In fact, they would probably fight *against* the Federation, which would cost us a lot o' lives."

"Well someone needs to do something," Kimberly said. She crossed her arms over her chest. She refused to accept that nothing could be done to help these people."

"Maybe ye can, lass, after all this is over. Ye can lead a revolution!"

"Is that sarcastic?" Could she? Could she start a revolution? Maybe the rebels could help her with that after they completed her mission.

Or perhaps she could inspire them to do more or lobby for more funding for them.

"If ye couldn't tell then that tells me yer serious about this."

"Not serious. Just...passionate."

"Bah, passion. Passion fades like the wind in time. Passion is overrated."

"It sounds like you speak from experience."

Corbin waved his hand. "Eh, tis a tale for another day."

Kimberly made a mental note to ask him about it another day.

The town of Vortville emerged out of the smog. They passed the city limits, identified by a faded sign that read "welcome to Vortville," and hovered down Main Street.

"Second street on the right," Baillidh called out from the back seat. He was their navigator for this mission.

"Oi see it," Corbin said, slowing down as they neared the second street and turned down it.

"There should be a warehouse at the end of this street."

"There be warehouses all around us," Corbin pointed out. Indeed, on both sides of the street massive warehouses created artificial walls and the shadows created by their obstruction of the sun caused the headlights of the hover car to trigger.

"There's one at the end of the street," Baillidh insisted.

Indeed, the street ended at a warehouse that looked much like the others around it. Several vehicles were parked out in front of it. "I think this is the place," Kimberly said.

The trio departed their car and approached the building. Corbin drew his sidearm. "What are you doing?" Kimberly asked.

"Being prepared, lass."

"These are allies."

"Never hurts ta be prepared."

Kimberly rolled her eyes but drew her pistol anyway, just in case.

They neared the door and Kimberly slowed her pace. The door was ajar. "That doesn't look good."

"Maybe they just didn't fix the lock," Corbin suggested. "Tis a pretty run-down area o' town."

She looked back at Corbin. "Really? Sarcasm at a time like this?"

Corbin flashed her a smile. "We dun know what 'time' this is. Could be nothin.'"

Kimberly shook her head and faced forward. "I'm waiting for you to gloat that you were right."

"Oi'll wait till we're inside before I gloat." She imagined him smirking.

Kimberly inspected the door. A hole in the center looked to be caused by a coilgun shell. She felt a sinking feeling in her stomach. She lifted her pistol higher and pushed the door open with her foot. The lights were off and she heard no sound. A smell assaulted her nose, however - the smell of rotting flesh. She found a light switch next to the door and flipped it on. At first all she saw was racks filled with boxes. She made her way further in and the smell intensified. She turned a corner and shrieked before turning to dry heave back the way she'd come.

Corbin, who had been right behind her, rushed around the corner and said, "Shit, that's a lot o' blood."

Kimberly composed herself and looked up. Baillidh stood there watching her. "I don't even want to know," he said.

"Stay here," Kimberly said. "Keep watch." She turned, covered her nose with the sleeve of her jacket and went back around the corner, this time steeling herself for what she knew was there.

Bodies, lots of bodies, lay in a mangled heap in the center of the room. Body parts lay strewn around the mound. Kimberly couldn't even begin to count how many bodies there were for certain, but she guessed at least forty. "Is this...? Is this the resistance?"

Corbin knelt by a corpse and picked up a bloody piece of cloth. A patch symbolizing the resistance still clung to it. "Oi'd say yes."

Kimberly came closer. "How did they die? What could have done this?" In the back of her mind she *knew* who did it, but she wanted Corbin to say it.

Corbin picked up a severed arm.

"Corbin! What are you doing?"

"Answerin' yer question." He brought it close to his face and studied it. "Looks like bite marks, like it twas chewed off." He tossed the arm aside and bent near the torso of another corpse. "Claw marks. Oi'd say the Krai'kesh."

Kimberly stared in horror at the arm. "Have some respect for the dead, Corbin. You don't just throw their arm on the ground."

"Sorry, m'lady, but I ain't much for believin' in an afterlife. No ghosts gonna haunt me for tossin' an arm. Did ye' hear what oi said about the Krai'kesh?"

A moan echoed through the warehouse.

Corbin jumped. "Wha' the 'ell was that?"

Despite the circumstances it was Kimberly's turn to chuckle. "Maybe it was that ghost of yours." She pointed toward a corridor opposite the side of the pile they came in on. "It sounded like it came from that way." She walked in that direction. "And yes, I heard you about the Krai'kesh. I was afraid of that. They were obviously compromised, but what's scarier is the Krai'kesh presence here, on the capitol of the Commerce Sector."

"Aye, suggests they're in bed with at least one of them houses."

"Baillidh, we're checking out the moaning noise. We'll be right back," she called out.

"All right, ma'am," Baillidh called back, voice shaking.

The moan came again. It had to be a survivor. A trail of blood caught Kimberly's eye. They followed it to a crate. She kept her pistol raised in case it was a trap or enemy who was wounded but when she leapt around the crate she lowered her pistol. "Got a survivor," she said to Corbin, who was standing several feet away watching her back. She turned her attention back to the survivor, who was a middle-aged woman with red hair and blue eyes. Blood coated her outfit and Kimberly realized her red hair was not red but blood-soaked brown hair. Both of her hands covered a blackened spot on her stomach. She scooted back when she saw Kimberly. "Ma'am, can you speak?"

The woman opened her mouth but only a moan came out. Her wide eyes darted between Kimberly and Corbin and she emitted a whimper next.

"There's nothing to be afraid of. We're here to help." Kimberly holstered her pistol and knelt. She extended her hand. "Let me help."

The woman shook her head. "No... nothing...can...help...us...now." The broken words came out in a tremble.

Sensing the woman's time was short Kimberly decided to get right to the point. "Who did this to you? What happened here?"

"We   were...meeting,"   she   strained   to   speak. "When...creatures...surrounded...us.   Killed...everyone.   I... buried...crawled out."

"Creatures surrounded you, killed everyone and you were buried under the pile of corpses and crawled out?" Kimberly repeated. "Is that what happened?"

The woman nodded weakly.

Kimberly shared a look with Corbin. He nodded. They were right. She looked back at the woman. "Were any humans with them?"

"Don't...know. Thought...saw...someone...back."

"Hmmm." She was an unreliable witness who may not have seen what she thought she did in the heat of the moment.

"Do you know how they found you?"

"Agent...from...Tar...Ebon...coming...here.   Betrayed...us. Only...explain..." She ceased speaking and began coughing up blood.

"No," Kimberly said, shaking her head. "No, we didn't...I would never." She took a deep breath. "We did not betray you."

"You're...agent?"

"Yes, from Tar Ebon."

"Then...how?"

How had they been betrayed? That was what this woman wanted to know, the same as Kimberly. "I don't know, but we're going to get to the bottom of this. We're going to get you help, just hang on."

"No. Let...me...die," she said. "Going...to...better..." She stopped speaking, let out one final breath, and her eyes glazed over.

Kimberly reached out and closed her eyelids. Corbin wore a sad expression when she looked at him. "Are you okay?" she asked.

Corbin cleared his throat, shook his head and looked her in the eyes. "Oi will be, lass. Oi've seen worse, bad as that sounds."

"She thought they were betrayed," Kimberly said. "But we didn't betray them. So who did?"

"Someone else in the FIA, oi'd guess."

A traitor? In the FIA? No, it couldn't be. "FIA operatives are vetted in-depth. Who would betray us? Who even knew of our mission? Only Isabelle, and she wouldn't betray us."

"No, oi don't think she would, but others *did* help us. Someone had ta create our identities and get us on that transport. Someone had ta arrange lodging fer us. All o' them steps create opportunities fer loose ends and flappin' tongues."

Kimberly shook her head. "No, there has to be another explanation."

"Why are ye so doubtful? The Cult of Rae already showed they could infiltrate the FIA, or have ye fergotten Crossroad Station?"

"I haven't forgotten it. I just..." Her shoulders slumped. "I just don't want to believe it."

"Ye don't want ta admit how corrupt the FIA could be," Corbin observed.

Kimberly nodded. A thought came to her. "If someone knew about us and our meeting and sent the Krai'kesh here, are they coming after us next?" She imagined trying to re-enter the civilized part of the planet and being ambushed or held after an anonymous tip and imprisoned. Sweat ran down her back at the thought.

"Can't worry 'bout that now, lass. Let's just get back ta the embassy. Who knows, they may have found the rebels on their own, no informant needed."

"You're just trying to make me feel better."

"Is it workin'?"

Kimberly cracked a smile. "It's showing your soft side, which makes me feel a little better."

Corbin cleared his throat. "Yeah, well, dun get used ta it."

The two of them returned to the mound of bodies and found Baillidh where they had left him. His attention was focused on his datapad and he jumped when he noticed them. So much for being a lookout. "Let's go, we have what we need."

"Was it a survivor?" Baillidh asked.

"Yes, but she died. She claimed someone in the FIA betrayed them. She thought it was us. Absurd, right?"

Baillidh paled.

"Not necessarily, ma'am."

"What do you mean?" Kimberly said in a more intense voice than intended.

"I was fiddling with my datapad because its power usage was high and the battery was draining faster than expected. So I was digging into the code and..."

"Spare us the details, Baillidh. What's your point?"

"There was a bug in my datapad."

"A *bug*?"

"Yeah, you know, a virus, program designed to harm or..."

"I know what it is. But how did *you* of all people not detect it?" She didn't suspect Baillidh of espionage. Only a stupid spy would rat on themselves.

"Hubris, ma'am. I thought my device uncrackable. I didn't scan it for viruses thoroughly enough."

"Where was it transmitting from?"

"It looks like it transmitted once we arrived on the surface of the planet."

"What was the destination?"

"So far as I can tell...the embassy."

"The Federation embassy?" was the only thing Kimberly could say.

"Yes. I can't pinpoint it further than that without direct access to their server rooms to determine where the signal was routed once on the intranet but it definitely terminated at the embassy."

"Bloody 'ell," Corbin said. "So there be a traitor at the embassy?"

"It would appear so."

"Well, do we go back or do we try our luck out here?"

"If we *don't* go back we'll look more suspicious than if we do go back," Kimberly said. "Clearly whoever the spy is wants us alive for some reason or we'd have been ambushed by now."

"Dun jinx us. Still some ways ta go before we're *safe* in the embassy again."

"Let's go back and we can make a plan at that time. It will give Baillidh time to infiltrate the Federation intranet and figure out who the mole is."

"That won't be easy," Baillidh warned. "I have to physically access the server room. Even if I had my actual credentials as an agent I wouldn't be allowed in without top-level clearance. And revealing my actual identity would probably tip off the mole."

"Right, so we keep our identities a secret at all costs. We find which corporation is working with the Krai'kesh and infiltrate them."

"I dunno if we *want* ta find that information, lass."

"It's what Isabelle sent us here to do."

"Oi know. It's just...oi like all me limbs."

Kimberly gaped at him. "You just walked into a bloodbath without flinching and you're complaining about fighting Krai'kesh?"

"Them weren't me limbs laying out there. I'm awfully attached to me limbs."

"Well if you don't go along with my plan I'll rip your limbs off myself," Kimberly said, half-joking.

"Kinky."

"Let's go, before I castrate you here and now."

Chapter 10- Patience is a Virtue

A void portal opened and the *Dauntless* passed through. John raised the shields and Derek studied the sensor display, looking for hostile threats. He half-expected to hear target lock alarms or proximity alarms, but instead was met with a scene of carnage.

Pieces of ships floated through space, forming a miniature asteroid field of metal debris that circled Proxima X.

John whistled softly. "Well, something went down here."

"Yes, but what?" Ashley asked. "I don't see any Krai'kesh remains, only human ships."

"So maybe it truly was pirates?" Derek asked. "A large enough force to overwhelm the defenses?"

"It could be," John said. "The deutronium mines are a high value target. Pirates could have taken advantage of the situation to try to make a power grab." He laughed. "Ha-ha, I made a pun."

Derek quirked an eyebrow. *I'm surprised he knows what a pun is*, he thought

"Well, if it was pirates, they stuck around to operate the mine," Ashley pointed to a spot on the display and zoomed in. A large ore ship was docked at a station orbiting the moon Proxima X but showed no damage. A pair of fighters flashed past it but did not fire.

"Are they displaying a signature?" John asked.

"If I ping them they'll know we're here," Derek pointed out.

"Son, they already know we're here if they have any kind of sensors. Void portals aren't exactly subtle."

"Right," Derek said, blushing. He tapped a few times on the screen before responding. "They're listed as belonging to House...Artois." He felt so shocked he almost hadn't gotten the last word out.

"That doesn't make sense," Ashley said. "The briefing Admiral Rigsby passed on to us said House Vivendi owns the moon and runs the mines. What is House Artois doing here?"

"I have a feeling we're about to find out," John said, pointing to where the pair of fighters had turned and were speeding toward them.

"Attention unauthorized freighter. You have entered restricted property owned by Artois Industries. Leave now or we will be forced to take action against you."

"Hey there, gents," John said. "We were just passing through. Maybe you can help us. We're looking for someone. My daughter, in fact, Emma Edgerton. She's a pilot in the Federation. Have you seen her?"

The previous speaker did not respond but instead closed the link. Missile lock alarms sounded as the enemy fighters came within range. "I guess that's a no." Two pairs of missiles streaked toward the *Dauntless*.

"Or they do know and they don't want to tell us," Ashley said.

"Well, we'll just have to be persuasive," John said as he targeted one of the missiles and fired the forward lasers. It exploded. He targeted the next and fired. He opened a link to Ethan. "Ethan, can you take a turret and send one of your boys to the other turret?"

"On it. And I'll send one of my *men* to the other turret."

"Men, boys, it's all the same."

"Except it's not."

"Listen to your father. He knows things."

"Like how to speak in the third person? So wise." He closed the link.

"Kids," John lamented as he targeted the third missile and fired. "I liked it better when he was ten."

"Why, because he was shorter?"

"And more agreeable, yes."

"I don't know what son you remember, but he was always a typical boy. Stubborn, disobedient, and bull-headed."

"While Emma was a perfect angel? I don't think so, dear."

"She was corrupted by her brother."

"Okay, apologist." John destroyed the fourth missile before turning to her and winking.

Can we focus on the approaching hostile fighters please? Derek thought. "Uh, guys, how about we fight these buggers off and reminisce later."

"Good idea, kid." He turned back to the console. "Only two fighters. Should be a walk in the park."

As he spoke, a dozen more fighters streaked out of the station the transport was docked at.

"Geeze, where's the wood to knock on when I need it." He activated the ship intercom. "We've got more company. Make sure you're all strapped in back there."

"Just don't mention the Krai'kesh, dear," Ashley said. "We wouldn't want *them* to show up too."

"Yeah, I think I'll just keep my mouth shut."

The first two fighters closed to laser range. They were not equipped with coilguns. The shields absorbed the first volley of lasers with ease. The top and bottom quad-linked coilgun batteries made quick work of them. "Damn, I almost feel sorry for those chaps. Almost," John said.

Derek snorted. "Those dozen fighters are probably saying the same thing about us right about now."

"Oh come on. We've faced worse odds than this."

"Those are Z-3000 fighters coming toward us, John. Not like the antiques we just vaped."

John shrugged. "Yeah, so?"

Ashley pointed a finger at him. "I seem to recall you drooling over them last year at the galactic spacecraft show."

John groaned. "That was before they were trying to kill me. Nothing kills admiration faster than that. No pun intended."

He really likes puns, Derek thought.

"Okay, now I need quiet. Let me concentrate on doing awesome things."

"Should we leave the cockpit then?" Ashley asked, starting to rise from her chair.

"No, no, I need an audience." His hand squeezed the yoke and he leaned forward. "Here we go!"

The dozen fighters flew in a wedge formation, all of them with a clear line of fire. As expected, twenty-four missiles accelerated toward the *Dauntless*.

"Ashley, would you be a doll and create a magnetic storm?"

"Really, that's your plan? Ask me to do something I haven't done in two centuries?"

"Would you rather we blow up?"

Ashley sighed. "Fine. Launch a missile."

John clicked a button on the yoke. "Missile away!"

Ashley leaned back in her chair. Derek assumed she was closing her eyes. He watched the missile streak out straight through space, no target in mind. It neared the cluster of hostile missiles. It passed beneath them and something miraculous happened. The enemy missiles ceased accelerating and followed the missile John launched. His missile continued forward, incidentally toward the dozen enemy fighters, followed by a gaggle of deadly missiles tumbling end-over-end.

"What is that?"

"Magnetic storm," John explained, leaning back and putting his hands behind his head as if to take credit for Ashley's accomplishment. "Ashley uses the missile as a focal point for a magnetic field. It swirls around the missile and draws in anything metal that is similar size or smaller than the object."

"Wow, I'm impressed. She should do that more often."

"I'm...going...to...beat...you...both," Ashley said in between breaths. "Not...easy."

"Oh come on, you created an asteroid whirlwind, how hard can a magnetic field be?"

Ashley turned toward John, opened her eyes and gave him a glare. The enemy missiles started to falter in their following of the *Dauntless's* missile.

John held up his hands. "Okay, okay, I'll be nice. Just keep," he waved toward the missiles, "them going, will you? Please."

"You owe me," Ashley said before leaning back again in her chair. The missiles resumed their trajectory and continued a direct intercept course with the enemy fighters.

The enemy fighters decided at that moment firing more missiles was a good idea. Two dozen more missiles streaked out, but were subsequently affected by the magnetic storm. They flew straight toward the oncoming missile and then spun around it.

The enemy Z-3000s scattered, likely realizing what was next, but it was too late. The lone missile exploded and in turn the other missiles orbiting it exploded as debris hit it. A ring of fire, debris and death expanded. A swath of debris collided with the first of the oncoming fighters and ripped it apart. The missiles which continued to follow the magnetic storm slammed into several of the fighters, exploded, and added their debris to the spinning disc of death. At last the storm dissipated, and the pieces of debris went flying away from the epicenter, slamming at high speed into the remaining fighters and destroying several. Only one enemy fighter remained, and it flew back toward the station.

Ashley sat forward and turned her head toward John. "Did that satisfy you, *dear*?"

"Uh, yeah," John said. "That'll work."

"'That'll work?' That's all I get?"

"Well, you let one escape."

Ashley punched John on the shoulder.

"Ow!"

"I'm going to punch more than your shoulder if you don't apologize."

"Sorry, you did great, babe. I was just joking."

"Uh huh, sure you were."

The *Dauntless* continued toward the station orbiting Proxima X. No further fighters emerged to face them and the station did not fire on them. Either the fight had gone out of them or they had no weapons with which to fire on the *Dauntless*. Derek thought it looked worse for wear.

They flew right into the docking bay. The lone fighter which had challenged them sat there but no humans were in sight. "Way to roll out the welcome mat, House Artois. Your girlfriend needs to teach these guys some manners, Derek."

"She's estranged from her house," Derek reminded John.

"I can see why. He clicked on the comm. "Ethan, you and your boys, I mean men, might want to gear up. There's no welcome party, which makes me suspect a trap is waiting for us."

"Way ahead of you," Ethan responded. "We're already geared up, since you didn't let us shoot at anything but those first two antiques."

"Hey, sharing is caring. I wanted to share some kills with your mother. Wouldn't want to inflate your ego further by letting you say you single-handedly took on like half a dozen fighters by yourself."

Ethan snorted. "You coming with us?"

John stood up from his seat. "Sure, why not." He looked to Derek and Ashley. "You two in?"

Derek nodded. "Of course, sir."

"I'm going to lie down and take a nap," Ashley said, also rising. "Wake me if something important happens."

"Like if we all die from a booby trap?"

"You better not all die from a booby trap. But yes, that would be an important situation."

John gave her a thumbs up. "Got it, babe."

The ramp lowered and John, Derek, Ethan, and his Marines tromped down the ramp, weapons at the ready and combat suits active. Even John wore his combat suit. They reached the door leading out of the docking bay. Of course it didn't slide open. "Locked us out, eh?" John said. He tilted his head toward the door. "Got anything for this?"

"Rico, blow it," Ethan ordered. He, Derek, and the other Marines lined up further down the wall.

John stood next to Rico as he placed a small explosive charge before jerking into motion. "Oh, right. Explosives." He came to stand behind Derek.

A muted *pop* indicated detonation and two Marines used the hole in the door as a hand-hold to shove the door open. Once the door was propped open the others slid inside. Ethan deactivated the door using the interior controls.

"Why didn't we just hack the outside console?" John asked.

"It's faster to blow shit up," Ethan said, proceeding down the corridor.

"Yeah, I suppose it is at that," John agreed.

The group continued through the corridors toward where they presumed the command center was. They met no resistance whatsoever. No booby traps, no defenders, nothing. "This place is giving me the creeps," John said. "Like that haunted house feel."

"They're obviously consolidating their forces," Ethan said. "Rather than allowing us to divide and conquer."

"Or they're huddling in fear of us."

"I doubt it."

"It was a joke, lighten up, son."

Ethan let out a sigh but didn't speak except to say, "this should be the corridor we're looking for." He turned left down the corridor. "The door should be...shit..." He leapt back around the corner as laser fire filled the space he'd just occupied, slamming into the wall to their right. "There's their reinforcements. "Happy?"

"What have they got?" Derek asked.

"Laser gat," Ethan said. "Two of them. Plus about a dozen security troops behind those."

"Well, are we gonna keep them waiting or what?" John asked.

Ethan extended a hand. "Be my guest."

John interlocked his fingers and stretched his arms in front of him. "Stand back and prepare to be amazed." He stepped out into the line of fire. The first beams of light slammed into a shield of light in front of him like water spraying against a rock. More beams followed but none pierced the veil of light. In fact, the shield grew brighter. Then it expanded and flowed down the hallway. Screams of pain silenced a moment later then echoed down the hallway. He peeked around the corner. "There we go."

Derek followed the others around the corner. Burnt corpses littered the end of the hall, two mangled together with the laser gats they had died operating. Ash in the shape of men clung to the door at the far end.

"What's our breaching method of choice?" John asked. "Explosives? Beam of light? Hacking?"

"We've been over this," Ethan said. "None of us are hackers. You can't do a beam of light with no sunlight unless you absorb a lot of energy. So that leaves us with explosives." He motioned to one of his Marines and they rushed forward to place four shaped charges against the door. They ran back and hit the detonator. Four fountains of fire shot out toward the group of Federation forces and the opening the explosion formed toppled inward. The way to the bridge was clear.

Let's see what else might await us, Derek thought. The group approached along the side of the corridor, weapons raised. No weapon fire or explosives came through the opening, nor did shouts of alarm emanate from the hole.

"Gas," Ethan ordered.

One of the Marines tossed a smoke grenade into the room. Smoke billowed out of the hole in the blast door.

"Infrared."

Derek switched on the infrared function of his helmet and followed Ethan inside. At first he saw nothing, no heat signatures at all. But then a head popped up from behind a console and a red burst blinded him for a moment as they fired. The shot went wide and hit the intact portion of the blast door. Derek's targeting interface compensated for the brightness and he returned fire, lighting up the console and forcing the enemy to take cover.

Unfortunately, they were not the only enemy combatant. More popped out from behind other consoles or nooks and fired as well. A muted grunt from his left suggested one of the Marines with them had been struck.

"Keep one of them alive," Ethan shouted.

Derek spotted a man in a pilot uniform and fired. They dropped.

The firefight was over in minutes with most of their opponents dead and two wounded. The two survivors were bound up and dragged back to the docking bay where they were forced to their knees.

Ethan stood in front of them and looked back and forth. "Now which one of you are going to tell me where Emma Edgerton went?"

"Who?" one of the men said quickly. Too quickly.

"One of the pilots of Victory Squadron. Where is she?"

The man who spoke looked sidelong at his companion.

Ethan withdrew his pistol and aimed it at the head of the silent man. "Whoever tells me what I want to know first gets to live."

Derek squirmed. He didn't agree with that type of threatening, but he did not attempt to intervene. Today was not the day for good cop bad cop.

The man who spoke originally held up his hands. "All right, all right, I'll tell you what I know." He took a deep breath. "We arrived with the fleet and took over the station. I don't know much about what went on in space but I did hear some Federation pilots were captured. The Krai'kesh arrived and took off and the rest of the fleet left after that."

"The House Artois fleet?"

"Yes, sir."

"And where was either fleet going?"

"I don't know."

"Back home, back home," the second man squealed. I remember because I wanted to be on the ship to return."

"And where is 'home,'" Ethan asked, clenching a fist.

"Epsilon III."

"And the exiled daughter of House Artois was with the Federation pilots," the first man said, trying to one-up the second man in knowledge.

Selene, Derek thought. "Did she get taken to Epsilon III?"

The first man shrugged. "As far as I know everyone was taken to Epsilon III."

Ethan studied them. Derek imagined him trying to determine if they were lying. "What was House Artois doing so far outside the Corporate Sector?"

"Hostile takeover, sir. We were liquidating House Vivendi's assets and acquiring their operation."

Ethan groaned. "I always hated merchant-speak."

"Why do you think your uncle waged a war on them at one point?" John asked. "I mean, it takes a lot to make Jason angry, but they succeeded."

Ethan clenched his fist but lowered his pistol. "I can see how. All right, throw them both in the brig."

"Wait, you're not going to kill us?" the first man asked.

"Do you want to die?" Ethan asked.

"N...no," the second man said.

"Then stop questioning why we're letting you live." He waved at them. "Get them out of my sight." Two Marines dragged them aboard the *Dauntless*.

The group boarded and made their way to the bridge.

Contrary to her word, Ashley was not sleeping in her bunk but had fallen asleep in the co-pilot's chair. She awoke with a start as the door opened. "Oh, you're back. That was quick."

"Not many defenders," Ethan reported.

"And I did some awesome light magic stuff," John said.

Ashley patted John's arm while rolling her eyes after he was seated. "I'm sure you did, dear. Did you find the information you needed?"

Ethan spoke, "The idiots didn't know much, except where the traitor fleet went. And that the Krai'kesh were here."

"That seems like a lot. The Krai'kesh are working with the merchant families?"

"House Artois at least."

"Where did they go?"

"Back home to the Epsilon system."

Ashley cursed. "How are we going to get into the capitol of the Commerce Sector?"

"I'll figure something out," John said. "Don't worry."

"I'm going to worry until my baby girl is found," Ashley said.

"At least we know she isn't dead," Derek pointed out.

"Ethan said they were idiots. How would they know if she was killed and dumped out an airlock or not."?

Her somber words dampened the mood in the room.

"We don't know for sure," Ethan began, "but it's a good guess they wouldn't needlessly kill an Eternal. If anything, they would use her as a bargaining chip to blackmail the Federation or something."

"True," Ashley agreed. "Well, what are we waiting for? Let's get to the Epsilon system."

"Here we go," John said and flew the *Dauntless* out of the docking bay.

Chapter 11 - Family Reunion

A void portal opened and the *Goldstar* emerged in the space above Epsilon III. Selene watched through the viewport as the planet neared and a feeling of dread settled in her stomach. Not dread for her - dread for the fate of Emma. What would the Krai'kesh do to her? Would they ever see each other again? The thought kept her from touching the fancy tray filled with food the servant brought earlier before exiting and re-locking the door.

The door to her cell opened with a swish. "The Lord Artois has requested your presence in the docking bay," a guard said. It wasn't a request.

Selene took her time turning to face the guard, who was standing in the doorway. He did not carry stun cuffs but held a stun baton at the ready. There went her thoughts of escaping. She looked down at her attire. Her freshly laundered flight suit clung to her. She could not say her brother was inhospitable. Servants at her beck and call, any food, drink or service she desired. Everything except her freedom. Her brother had not dined with her again after the night of her outburst. In fact, he hadn't contacted her at all.

The guards led Selene to the docking bay where her brother was dressed in a formal dress uniform, the logo of House Artois embroidered on his chest. His position in the family granted him an honorary captain's rank, though he had served no military time. She doubted he could even use a pistol with skill. He smiled when he saw her. It sent a shiver down her spine. "There you are." He frowned at her uniform. "You're wearing *that* hideous outfit?"

"Yes. As a reminder of who I am and that I am a prisoner here." She was tempted to recite her name, rank, and serial number any time she was asked to speak while on Epsilon III but decided against it. She was not a prisoner of war, for the Federation and Commerce Sector were not at war. Would anyone even come for her, a lowly pilot?

He pursed his lips. "I should have had the servants burn it instead of launder it. You are not a prisoner, dear sister."

"The locked door said otherwise."

He tutted. "A safety precaution, that's all. I didn't want any of the crew getting any ideas and trying to harm you."

"Mmmm hmmm," Selene said, not buying any of his bullshit. "I presume you asked me here because we are going down to the planet now?"

"Yes, Father wants to see you right away."

Selene rolled her eyes. "I bet he does. Am I *free* to say no to the invitation to see him?"

"Why would you want to do that?" He cocked his head to the side.

Gee, I don't know, because the bastard disowned me? Instead she said. "He's probably a very busy man and doesn't have enough time to see me."

"Actually, he has a one hour block of time set aside for you."

"How generous."

"I thought so."

Of course you did, Selene thought.

The guards ushered her toward the transport and she stomped aboard. Her brother followed her into the transport and it took off toward the surface of the planet. She couldn't help but look out the viewport while they descended - it was better than staring at her brother or the floor. The world hadn't changed. The cities were still where she remembered, the poor still lived in their ghettos surrounding the cities. If anything, the ghettos had spread out further while the towers had gotten taller, if that were possible.

"Does it bring back memories?" her brother asked.

It did, though probably not the memories he was thinking of. Unbidden memories rose in her mind. Memories of scampering through the streets of the city and sneaking out through old sewer pipes into the ghetto. Some of her best friends had lived there. Until her father found out and walled the pipes up. He would have wiped out her friends too if Selene hadn't begged her mother to intervene, an action which had earned her mother a beating. But her father had relented after realizing what he had done to his wife. She looked at her brother for the first time since entering the transport. "Yes. We were so naive." Her mother did her no favors shielding her from her father until she was older. It only caused more shock when she learned her father was not a busy but caring father and was instead a busy cold-hearted bastard who ruled her mother through fear, intimidation, and threats.

Silence returned to the shuttle and minutes later they landed at the private landing pad jutting out of the side of Artois Tower, near the top. A dozen honor guards wearing ceremonial open-face metal helmets, armor, and cloaks awaited her brother's return. They certainly weren't there for *her* benefit. Her brother descended the ramp first. The guards saluted him.

Selene followed, the two guards who had accompanied her from the *Goldstar* behind her. Did they think she would run *now*, with nowhere to run? The honor guard did not react to her presence and lowered their arms, though one remained saluting a few seconds longer than the others. They probably didn't even recognize her. She tried to avoid looking at them for fear she would recognize some of them from the past but her eyes drifted to the one who had been slow to cease saluting. She found a grizzled face, gray beard and gray eyes looking at her in return. The man gave an imperceptible nod. Selene racked her brain, trying to place the face, but could not in that moment. She did maintain eye contact and return the nod, though.

The honor guard fell in behind Selene and her brother as they passed into the Tower. Polished crystal floors reflected the glow lamps hanging from the ceiling and their footsteps echoed due to the vaulted ceilings. They walked for a few minutes before her brother turned to the right at an intersection. Selene followed and ascended steps to where two massive doors stood closed. The guards pushed them open as they approached and Frederick strode into the throne room as if he owned the place. Perhaps he would, one day.

The throne room. A pompous declaration of power from a by-gone era. Her father fancied himself a king, though a king among seven other kings in the Commerce Sector. The throne room reflected his tastes in the black stone pillars and walls that seemed to suck happiness from the air. Selene immediately felt a bleakness within her.

A throne room wouldn't be complete without a throne, of course. At the far end of the room her father occupied his throne. He looked older, with a full head of gray hair and a gray beard, but, as she neared, she saw his eyes were still the same cool, analytical, callous eyes she had come to know all too well.

"Father," Frederick said, kneeling. "Thank you for seeing us. I know you are busy. Selene has returned."

Her father flicked his eyes from Frederick to Selene, his face impassive.

Selene resisted the urge to squirm, or to say something. What would she say? What *could* she say? Thoughts of reciting her name, rank and serial number rose again. Better to keep her walls up than let them down and allow the chief negotiator of her family exploit her.

"So my errant daughter returns," he rumbled. "Have you come to apologize for your insubordination and beg my forgiveness?"

She was surprised he acknowledged her as his daughter. She took a deep breath. "No, Father. I am here as a prisoner of my own House, against my will."

Her father nodded. "I assumed as much. You wear the markings of the Federation," he observed.

Selene puffed up her chest a little. "I am an officer in the Federation and a fighter squadron leader."

"She accompanied the Federation force which arrived during our takeover of the Vivendi property, Father," her brother explained. "We neutralized the squadron she was in,"

"You mean murdered my squad-mates before my eyes," Selene interjected.

"And brought her here when our allies wanted nothing to do with her."

"It would have been better for you to throw her to the Krai'kesh, Frederick."

"Father...I thought you would be pleased," Frederick stammered.

Her father turned an angry gaze upon Frederick and clenched his fists. "Why would I be pleased, you fool? I disowned her and banished her. Yet here you are, dragging her back as if she is still my daughter. I should string you up for your stupidity, but I will save the rope."

Dear old dad, Selene thought, *always thinking about the savings. He didn't become a trillionaire overnight,* she reminded herself. "If you let me go, Father, I will be happy to depart from this place."

Her father's gaze turned icy again as he glared at her. "No. I promised you when I banished you that you would face death if you returned. Your brother may have brought you back but the result is the same. You will remain here as my prisoner until your punishment can be carried out."

A bead of sweat dripped down her forehead. Her father was going to kill her? For certain? "Father, you can't..."

Her father swiped with his hand. "Enough! Guards, take her to the dungeons. There will be no lavish accommodations in *my* house for traitors."

Two guards, one of them the one with the gray beard, came up next to her and pulled her away. She resisted and shouted "*You* are the traitor! You betrayed all mankind to the Krai'kesh. How could you?"

Her father held up his hand to forestall the guards. "You petulant child. Our house is a house of survivors. We survived every war between the Federation and the Empire or between the Federation and *anyone* by being *useful* to the winning side while remaining neutral and taking from our rivals when the opportunity presented itself. It is a logical analysis that the Krai'kesh will win this war. I am siding with the winner, daughter, and you and anyone who stands in their way will be crushed."

"And what then?" she asked. "When the Federation and Empire lie in ruins you don't think the Krai'kesh will come for you?"

"They have promised me all the planets I desire in exchange for my aid."

"And you trust them?"

"More than the Federation which banished us to this corner of the galaxy."

"Because of our greed! We nearly tore the Federation apart once before. Of *course* they would banish the merchant families!"

Her father waved away her observation. "Bah. What's done is done. The Krai'kesh will soon stand victorious and House Artois will stand with them. Take her away."

At first Selene dug in her heels, forcing them to drag her, but finally she got her feet under her and turned to face the direction they were going. "I can walk," she snapped. "And I know the way." She turned her head as she walked. "Your arrogance will be your undoing, Father."

"Perhaps, Daughter, but you will not live to see such a thing."

Selene went to the elevator and descended to the basement level, the guards watching her like a hawk. They were waiting for her to make a move so they had an excuse to rough her up. She knew their types. The dungeons hadn't changed since she was a child running down those halls. Artificial black stone covering durasteel supports lined the walls of the hallway. A cell on the left was empty. One of the guards pressed a button on the console next to the door and the force field deactivated. The other shoved her inside. The force field reactivated. Selene didn't bother touching it - she knew what the electrical shock emitted by those fields felt like after the time her brother locked her in a cell by accident.

A FEW HOURS LATER, as Selene tried to doze on the hard floor of her cell a voice came from the hallway. "Selene?"

She sat up. Her mother stood outside the force field, watching her with wide eyes. One of the guards, Ralph, stood to the side, watching her with suspicion. "Mother?" she asked with disbelief. "Is it really you?"

A tear slid down her mother's cheek and she gave a smile. "Yes, my darling, it's me."

"I would hug you but..." she beckoned to the field.

"I know, honey. I know. I will try to talk to your father, get you to better..."

"No," Selene said, her voice firm. "I will not have you risk your own life just to make mine a little more comfortable."

"I can't just stand by and watch my daughter die," her mother said.

Selene flicked her eyes toward Ralph and back to her mother. "What you're talking about is treason. My father decreed I am to die. Leave it alone, Mother."

Her mother's eyes went wide, but Selene believed she got the message. It wasn't safe to discuss the matter around the guard. She should have realized that, but she wasn't the savviest person in the galaxy. In fact, Selene's father had forbidden her mother from participating in knitting circles and other social gatherings with the other wives for fear she would undermine his strategies unwittingly after one disastrous occasion.

"I understand," she replied. "If you're resigned to it, I will say my goodbyes. You were always a bit odd, but I loved you. I pray you find peace in the after-life."

Was she truly saying goodbye? Had Selene's innuendo gone over her mother's head? Did she not realize she did *not* want to die but did not want to discuss treason with a guard present? Or was she being convincing for the sake of the guard. Selene couldn't tell. *It has been a long time away from home.*

"You were always kind to me, Mother. I'm sorry for being such a disappointment to you."

Her mother smiled sadly and shook her head as if to disagree with her. More tears streamed down her cheeks. No, Selene realized her mother was not ignorant - she did not want her daughter to die. She would do whatever it took, even lie, to save her daughter. "Good bye, Daughter." She turned and walked away.

The guard gave Selene another dirty glance before following her mother. Had he been convinced that her mother was resigned to her daughter's death or did he still harbor suspicions? Only time would tell.

A DAY LATER FREDERICK came to visit her. He awoke her from a restless sleep. "Hello, Selene. I trust you are being treated well."

Selene sat up and glared at him. "I haven't been raped yet, so there's that. But I would not call it being 'treated well.'"

Frederick cleared his throat. "Our guards do not rape prisoners. Regardless, I've spoken to Father."

You don't know your guards, then, Selene thought. More than one had eyed her with hungry gazes. She had not seen Artemis since the day before. "Has he agreed to let me live?"

"Sadly, no." He averted his eyes. "I've been sent to inform you of your execution date."

Selene took a deep breath. "Out with it, then. When am I to die?"

"Three days hence you will face a public execution in Steel Plaza."

"What will be the method? Hanging? Beheading? Poison?"

Frederick gaped. "We are not barbarians. It will be a dignified death by lethal injection."

Selene rolled her eyes. "I did say poison."

"Yes, but poison is such an... icky word."

"Oh, I'm sorry I offended your sensibilities," Selene scoffed. "I would offer to make reparations but I fear I will soon be dead."

A hint of sadness flashed across her brother's face but then he smiled. "It was nice knowing you, Selene. I'm sorry it had to be this way."

But it doesn't have to! Selene thought. She wanted to shout it at him, tell him what a fool he was and implore him to resist her father and advocate for her. If he and *her* mother both stood at her side her father would *have* to relent, wouldn't he? No, standing up to her father directly would get them both executed as well.

"So am I," was all she said.

"I really must go. I have an important appointment in ten minutes." He did not look at her. "Goodbye." He started walking away.

Selene did not bother saying anything. She couldn't bring herself to say goodbye, couldn't thank him for visiting and did not feel like insulting him further. She curled up and imagined Derek's face as she wished for sleep to come.

Chapter 12 - Vultures

"You're on with the president's office, sir," Zigana reported.

"This is Admiral Martin Rigsby. I need to speak with President Galantos immediately."

The woman on the other end of the holo looked as bored as the assistant of Admiral Hensen. What was with all the assistants being bored? "This is an unorthodox communication, Admiral. You should be going through official channels, which includes Fleet Command, before speaking with the Admiral."

"Please tell him this is a matter of national security," Martin said. "I cannot bring this to Fleet Command first."

The assistant sighed and Martin half expected her to roll her eyes. "May I ask what the matter is regarding?"

Martin hesitated. Yes, this was an assistant to the president, but who knew how many officials were in the pocket of the rogue elements within the Federation. "Tell him it involves the Supreme Commander and it is critical."

The woman quirked her eyebrow. Did she doubt his word? Did she think he was lying and just dropping the Supreme Commander's title for no reason? "One moment, Admiral, while I speak with the president. The link went black as she muted the line. Several minutes passed. Did that bode well or ill? At last the assistant returned to view. "I'm putting you through to the president. I would like to remind you he is a very busy man. Do not waste his time."

Martin bowed his head. "Of course. I wouldn't dream of it."

The image faded and was replaced with the youthful - compared to Martin, anyway - image of President Joseph Galantos. He wore his night black hair slicked back. He wore an amicable expression, though he did not smile. His green eyes took in Martin. "Admiral Rigsby, I presume?"

Martin offered a deep bow, bending at the waist. "President Galantos, thank you for taking my call."

"I was told you have critical information concerning the Supreme Commander?"

Martin breathed in deep. "Yes, sir. Have the Joint Chiefs contacted you yet?"

President Galantos frowned. "No. Why should they have?"

"I'm afraid I have bad news, sir. The Supreme Commander is missing in action."

The president's eyes grew wide. "Missing? What happened?"

"That is a sensitive matter, sir, and why I needed to speak with you personally. Are you alone?"

"Yes. Say what you need to say, Admiral."

"Our fleet was betrayed, sir. Rogue elements within the Federation fleet turned on us. They were supported by the Krai'kesh and appeared to be working with them." He held his breath. Would the president act in the same manner Admiral Hensen had? He hoped the president would not turn out to be a traitor.

The president narrowed his eyes and stroked his black beard. "That is troubling news, Admiral. You have proof of this, I presume?"

"Yes, sir. I have bridge recordings of one such traitor and sensor records of the space battle during which we were betrayed."

"Have you brought this to Fleet Command?"

"I have, sir. I brought it to the attention of Admiral Hensen." He looked away. "I'm afraid, however, sir, that Admiral Hensen may well be involved with the traitors."

"What? That is preposterous, Admiral. What makes you say such a thing?"

"I told him the name of a system my fleet and I were located in. I then sent a probe to that empty system. A fleet of Krai'kesh ships accompanied by the rogue ships appeared a short while later. The *only* person who knew I was 'in' that system was Admiral Hensen. It had to be him."

"Or it could be someone eavesdropping on his communications, could it not?"

Martin nodded his head in acknowledgment. "It is possible, sir, but unlikely. In my experience, such complicated explanations are incorrect. There is also the matter of Admiral Bordekov and several admirals earlier this week proposing to depose Dawyn as Supreme Commander. They were outvoted, but I fear the betrayal was the second part of their plan to bring down the Supreme Commander."

"These are dangerous allegations, Admiral. If what you are saying is true, our highest commanders are on the side of rebels."

"It would not be the first time, sir."

The president pursed his lips before speaking. "No, it would not be." He sighed in frustration. "Fine, I will have the Shadow Watch Guards investigate Admiral Hensen and any others you suspect of treason."

"That may be too late, sir. And it could tip your hand, making you a target. It is better for you to appear ignorant to the goings-on of the traitors"

"While I appreciate the sentiment, Admiral, I survived a Krai'kesh assault recently. I am not accustomed to backing down from a fight."

"Mr. President, if the traitors are as deeply embedded as we expect they will have eyes and ears everywhere. If they want to get to you, they *will*. And they will *want* to go after you if they sense you are close to uncovering their plans."

"I appreciate your concern, Admiral, but I am in the most secure building in the Federation, surrounded by the best security forces ever known. I think I will be okay."

"Need I remind you, sir, that you were betrayed by insurgents posing as Shadow Watch Guards in the past."

The president frowned but nodded. "Point taken. I will be in touch as the investigation progresses, Admiral. Godspeed."

Martin bowed his head once more. "And you, Mr. President." After the link closed Martin hung his head and sighed. "Oh, Zigana, I fear for his life."

"Why do you say that, sir?"

"He's too virtuous, too good, too naive. He thinks he is untouchable and that the rule of law will be on his side. These rebels will also have the law on their side, and they will make people like the president the evil ones. Those who do not learn from history are doomed to repeat it."

Zigana cocked his head to one side. "That is an ancient proverb, is it not?"

Martin snorted. "Yes, one of the original human sayings, I believe."

"I am surprised an ancient saying has been remembered but the missteps of the past have not."

Martin conceded that to Zigana. "Yes, I suppose that is ironic."

Chapter 13 -A Coup

A void portal opened and the *Renegade* passed through. Before Rachel sat the planet of Tar Ebon, the gem of the Federation. Thousands of ships swarmed around it, some entering, others departing. Traffic was so dense that shifting was only allowed in designated areas, usually far away from the planet, except for military vessels, which could shift near the poles. As the *Renegade* was not military they were starting far from the planet. "Don't be scared, Frank."

Frank scoffed. "You kidding me? I was dying for a challenge. I don't think I've seen this many ships in my entire life. Like a giant, fast-moving asteroid field."

Rachel rolled her eyes. "You get used to it."

"You've been here before, boss?"

Rachel stared at a button on the control panel. Memories surged upward from her subconscious. She closed her eyes, shoving them back down. "Yes. Years ago." *It was not pleasant*, she added mentally.

"Were you flying?"

It was Rachel's turn to scoff. "You know I can't fly worth crap, Frank. That's a damn silly question."

Frank smirked. "Just wanted to see if you were telling a tall tale, ma'am."

"I should make you swab the decks for that," she joked.

"But then who would fly the ship?" he asked.

"Maybe when we land," she said. She activated the internal comm. "Dear ol' Dad and aunt, can one of you please come to the cockpit and explain to me how we're going to *land.*"

"If I need to tell you how to land, we're in worse trouble than I thought," her father said. He was clearly trying to make a joke, but Rachel did not laugh, or say anything at all.

"Ignore my brother's awkward attempts at trying to reconnect with you. We're on our way." The channel closed.

Minutes later both Dawyn and Bridgette squeezed into the cockpit and took a seat.

Rachel turned to them. "Well, what's the plan?"

Dawyn closed his eyes for a moment. "I've just transmitted a series of codes to your console. Use those as authentication codes, in that exact order, and you'll be allowed through security with no difficulty."

Rachel frowned but looked to the console. "Secret codes? How come I didn't know about these?"

"They're secret for a reason," her father said dryly.

"And I was your daughter."

His face softened. "You still are. But the fewer people who knew about these codes the better. These were hard-coded into the authentication system as a bypass. We asked Jason to create them in the event something like this happened. We will likely only have a single use with them, however, for once the insurgents identify the code they will shut it down."

"That assumes the insurgents control Flight Control and can shut down codes," Bridgette said. "Why is it you're suddenly more cynical than *me*, Brother?"

"I'm not cynical," he replied. "I'm a realist."

"If you say so."

Rachel snapped her fingers. "Can we please focus on the matter at hand? What do we do once we're past security?"

"I will go to the FIA headquarters and gather as much intel as possible on the Cult of Rae," Bridgette said.

"You can't do it remotely?" Rachel asked.

Bridgette shook her head. "No. There is some information we cannot trust to the Shadownet, no matter how secure. The data is on air-gapped servers hidden deep inside my office. I'll just waltz in, grab the data and get out."

Rachel nodded. It sounded plausible. "Okay. What about you, Father? Are you going to run off also?"

Her father smirked. "Well, I am running off, but I need you and your team to accompany me."

"What's the mission?" she asked.

"I need to speak with the president. He may be the only person we know we can trust on this planet. I need to touch base with him and come up with a stop-gap to forestall the progress of these rebels."

"The Hague House is impenetrable. You're just going to walk in the front door?"

Her father's mouth dropped open and he put a hand to his chest. "I *am* still the Supreme Commander. That carries some weight." He brought his index finger and his finger to the point where they almost touched. "Just a little."

"Not on all matters," Rachel grumbled.

Her father gave her a sad look.

"Don't you think it would be better to like, sneak in?" Bridgette asked, breaking the silence. "Maybe through the secret entrance?"

Rachel's father nodded. "Yes, that's actually a good idea. The less attention we draw the better."

"First authentication prompt coming up. You got this, Rachel?"

Rachel nodded and turned back to the console again. She punched in the authentication code her father had given them. For a harrowing moment the screen was occupied by a spinning circle. But moments later a green "authenticated" message popped up. She let out a breath she didn't realize she had been holding. "One down," she counted the codes, "four to go."

They flew on toward Tar Ebon. "How does the authentication system work?" Rachel asked. "Is it random?"

"No. It is pre-designated at certain distances from Tar Ebon. The idea is that a nefarious element might pass the first authentication and do business on the surface of Helos, where the FIA can monitor them and keep them contained, but they won't likely pass the second authentication if they're serious criminals. If anyone fails an authentication beyond the first, the attention of the Home Guard is roused and fighters are dispatched to investigate and escort the offending vessel to an inspection checkpoint if necessary."

"So don't fail an authentication," Frank summarized. "Got it."

"Not if we want to maintain our stealth approach, no. If we're detected I can use my authority to call off the Home Guard but,"

"Yes, we know, the insurgents aboard the Home Guard vessels would find out you're alive and call back to their home base and suddenly your whole plan would be ruined, right?" Bridgette asked.

"I don't appreciate your tone, Sister," her father said. Rachel couldn't tell if he was joking or not.

"And your paranoia is wearing on me, Brother. It's like we've swapped bodies but you've brought out all the paranoia I usually keep under lock and key."

"It's not paranoia if there's evidence," her father rebutted.

"Then when we find this evidence I'll be the first to apologize," Bridgette said.

"Second authentication coming up," Frank announced. "We're being scanned."

"It's routine," Rachel's father replied. "Maintain your course and transmit the second authentication code."

Rachel did as she was bid. The second authentication code worked as well and they continued their course toward Tar Ebon. Three more security checks were also cleared and soon the *Renegade* passed the orbital ring and entered Tar Ebon's atmosphere.

"Where to now, Chief?" Frank asked, referring to Dawyn.

"Take us to Tar Ebon City. Docking bay thirteen at the Bard's Landing. I'm giving you the reservation code."

Rachel quirked an eyebrow. "You're really prepared for everything, aren't you? Did you foresee this or something?"

Her father shot a sidelong glance at Bridgette. "I have many contingency plans. It's one of the reasons I've lived this long."

"I'm going to FIA headquarters. Now," Bridgette announced. Her last word hung in the air as she disappeared into mist and the mist faded to a shadow.

"Why didn't she do that earlier?" Rachel said. "Like when we were flying in?"

"I'd like to say it was because of the riveting conversation, but alas that is not the case. The orbital ring around Tar Ebon emits a nullification field to create a barrier to shifting. Bridgette can overcome the barrier, but not without a great deal of energy."

Like when I slammed her against the wall, Rachel thought. "I see," was all she said.

The comm chimed. Rachel answered it. "What?"

"Hey boss, what's going on up there?" Reynaldo asked.

"We're going to meet the president of the Federation, so wear your best outfit."

"I always dress to impress, ma'am. It's Maggie you should be worried about."

A slapping sound came over the comm. "Thank you," Rachel said, assuming Maggie had hit Reynaldo in the back of the head or somewhere else.

"Us girls gotta stick together," Maggie said. "We'll gear up." The link closed.

The cockpit was quiet as Frank brought the *Renegade* in for a landing at Bard's Landing, dock thirteen. "Hey, isn't thirteen supposed to be an unlucky number?" Frank asked.

"Did that just dawn on you?" Rachel asked.

"Hey, I'm the pilot, not a scientist."

"It doesn't take a rocket scientist to remember that," Rachel grumbled.

"What was that?"

"Nothing. I was complimenting your sharp wit. We would never have known thirteen was an unlucky number without you, Frank."

"Oh well, just doing my...wait..." he turned his head toward her and narrowed his eyes. "You're being sarcastic, aren't you?"

Rachel smirked. "Yes, you big dummy. Now focus on landing."

"Shit, boss, I could land this old girl with my eyes closed."

"Please don't."

Frank laughed.

The landing gear engaged and a light jolt transferred from the floor up Rachel's legs as the *Renegade* met the ground. "Home sweet home," her father said.

Rachel shot him a dirty look. *Home was supposed to be where* I *was*, she thought. That had certainly not been Tar Ebon.

The trio exited the cockpit but Rachel shoved Frank backward. "You stay here with the ship, Frank. Keep her warm for us, in case we get into trouble."

Frank sighed. "Do I have to?"

"Yes, that's an order."

"But I've never seen Tar Ebon. I can't go roam the streets for like an hour."

"And risk getting lost and our ship not having a pilot. Hell no. You stay with the ship."

"Blah." He hung his head, feigning dejection, and walked back to the pilot's chair.

Rachel turned and was met with the sight of her father shaking his head and pointing at Maggie and Reynaldo, who had just emerged from the hallway. "No, you can't wear combat armor into the Hague House. Go change."

"But it's our combat armor," Reynaldo said, as if repeating what Rachel's father had just said would make a difference. "We need it." He paused as if waiting to see if realization would suddenly dawn on her father's face.

"If you wear combat armor into the Hague House you won't make it ten feet inside before you're swarmed by agents and probably shot because they think you're an assassin. The protocol says no combat armor inside the perimeter. I enacted that rule and not even I can override that. We have to be discreet."

Maggie grabbed Reynaldo by the shoulder, shot Rachel a dirty glance, and steered him back into the hallway. "We'll go change."

Why did she direct her gaze at me? Rachel wondered. It wasn't like she had any control over her father. What he said made perfect sense to her. Maggie and Reynaldo were just being difficult. Or were they jealous? She couldn't tell.

A few minutes later the duo returned in only their street attire with no combat armor in sight.

"Any weapons?" her father asked.

Maggie gaped. "We can't even carry concealed *weapons*?" Her face turned red.

Rachel's father cracked a smile. "Just kidding."

Maggie's face went slack, deadpan. Then she laughed out loud. "That's a good one, sir, because I was about ready to shoot you in the face, consequences be damned."

Rachel hit the button to lower the ramp and the four companions descended. No security or customs officials greeted them. "No welcome party?"

"I pay for discretion," her father explained. "The ship will be safe here and the company that runs this place won't ask questions."

"Smart," Rachel said.

"Wish we could do that," Reynaldo lamented.

"We can, it just costs us a hell of a lot more," Maggie said.

"How far are we from the Hague House?" Rachel asked.

"Three kilometers. But we're not going in the main entrance."

"There's a secret entrance?" Reynaldo said. "Sweet!"

"It's an ancient passageway that led into what was at the time the palace of the king of Tar Ebon. It was intended to be an escape tunnel in emergencies and a way for members of the royal family to leave the palace without public scrutiny - and sometimes even without their guards knowing. It's evolved since then and has better safeguards in place, but it still exists."

"'Safeguards?'" Maggie asked. "Like booby traps?"

"I prefer the term 'security measures.' But don't worry, I have the clearance codes to deactivate them."

They traveled out of Bards Landing, again without challenge, and down a nearby street crammed with people. Foreign travelers mingled with Tar Ebon natives in a cacophony of sounds that made Rachel's ears hurt. She found herself wishing for the solitude of deep space or the sparsity of far-flung destinations among the Non-aligned Planets. *Is it any surprise I don't like people? After how they treated me?* No, it shouldn't have come as a surprise. The physical wounds had healed from the beating she'd received and the angry mob had faced justice but the mental scars remained, making for restless nights.

The group turned down a dark alleyway. "Of course, it's always the dark alley," Reynaldo said. "Why are secret entrances always down a dark alley?"

"Because they're meant to be secret," her father said. He led them to the third door on the left. It was a black door, likely mage-forged. He knocked three times.

A moment passed before a sliding door covering the peep-hole opened. "Please state your name," a mechanical voice demanded.

"Dawyn Darklance."

"Authorization code?"

"Zero three seven alpha zed foxtrot."

The robot was silent for a few seconds. "Authorization code accepted. Welcome, Supreme Commander." The door swung inward. Inside a charging pad for the droid was the only furnishing. A pair of machine guns hung from the ceiling and pointed toward the door. She looked up to where another pair sat above the door, ready to shoot any intruders in the back should they try to rush the first pair in an attempt to bypass them. Holes in the wall suggested flamethrowers or other instruments of death. All to be expected for a secret passage giving direct access to the president's estate.

Her father seemed unperturbed by any of it. Hell, he'd probably designed it. "Thank you, ZB-8. Please deactivate security protocols in the passageway so my friends and I may pass."

"Of course, sir. One moment." Again the droid fell silent. "Security protocols are disengaged. The path is clear to enter the Hague House."

"Excellent. Thank you." Rachel's father led the way down the pathway which was now lit by light strips on the walls, floor, and ceiling. The lines of light stretched as far as Rachel could see.

"What sort of security protocols would there be?" Reynaldo asked.

Rachel's father pointed at the lines of light. "You see those? They're not just for illumination. In the event of a breach they activate lasers which stretch across the hall and from the ceiling to the floor. The wall panels can also retract, revealing more laser emitters. It can create a grid of lasers powerful enough to cut through combat armor, chopping a man into pieces."

"Sounds brutal."

"They've never had to be used. Yet."

The group continued down the hallway in silence before exiting and coming to a set of stairs. Rachel felt a chill down her spine and a pressure in her head. There, another pair of machine guns waited, this time one on each side as they exited the hallway. They really liked their machine guns, didn't they? "Couldn't a mage get through all these defenses?" Rachel asked.

"They could, except for the fact that right there is the start of the nullification field surrounding the Hague House."

Of course, Rachel thought. *That's what I felt. I forgot what it felt like.* The field would not affect her gravitational magic, but it did affect the elemental magic. "Yes, I just felt it go into effect."

He pointed to the stairs. "These stairs can also be electrified, making it extremely painful, even deadly, to ascend."

They ascended six flights of stairs before coming to a landing. There sat another black door. This door had a keyhole. Her father did not withdraw a key, however, but instead knelt and put his right eye in front of the hole. A light emanated from the hole and scanned his eye. A click sounded as the lock disengaged. He pulled open the door. "Piece of cake."

They passed through the door and found themselves in a lavishly furnished rectangular room with a window to the right. In front of them stood a dozen Shadow Watch Guards in full combat armor and with coilgun rifle aimed at them. "Stop right there. Hand where we can see them," one Guard commanded.

"Oh, *they* get combat armor," Reynaldo complained.

"Shut up," Rachel hissed, raising her hands in the air.

Her father raised his hands but did not appear concerned. "Lower your weapons. We are allies."

"State your identity," one of the Guards said.

"The door would have told you, as would ZB-8."

"State your identity," the Guard said again, raising his rifle a little.

Her father sighed. "Fine. I am Dawyn Darklance."

"We were told the Supreme Commander was dead. We will need to verify your identity."

"Told by who?"

"The president."

"Well I am very much alive. I need to speak with the president immediately."

"As I said, we need to verify your identity. I am going to fire a bullet at you."

Rachel frowned. Why were the Guards warning her father that he was going to shoot at him? Why was he going to shoot at him in the first place?

Her father nodded.

The Guard pulled the trigger on his rifle. The rifling made a zap noise as the bullet accelerated toward him faster than the eye could see.

Rachel considered using her gravity magic to slow the bullet, or stop it, but her father blurred and the bullet slammed into the black door behind him.

"Is that verification enough, Captain?"

The Guard nodded, lowered his gun and bowed. "Yes, Supreme Commander. Welcome to the Hague House. We will lead you to the president right away." He paused. "These are your...companions?" Rachel imagined him eying them dubiously.

"Yes. You may be familiar with my daughter, Rachel. And these are the crew members of her vessel, Reynaldo and Maggie. They are to be given the same treatment as me."

"Of course, sir. Right this way." The captain turned and led the group through a door behind him.

"What room is this?" Maggie asked for the first time since entering the secret passageway.

"It used to be a sitting room," Rachel's father explained as he passed a couch. "It still is, though it's rarely used any more."

"My uncle and aunt met in here," Rachel said.

"Really? Like for the first time?" Maggie asked.

"Yes. I'll tell you the story some time."

They followed the lead Guard into an oval room with a desk and two couches. The oval office.

A black-haired man sat behind the desk. He looked up as the group entered. He smiled and rose from his chair. "Dawyn, you're alive!"

Rachel's father bowed before the president. "Mr. President, it is a pleasure to see you again." Rachel assumed he bowed out of respect only, because his position was technically greater than any government official.

"What happened? I heard the *Nightblade* was destroyed. Was Admiral Rigsby lying?"

"No, sir. I trust Admiral Rigsby with my life and he was indeed telling the truth as he knew it. I actually prefer that I am presumed dead, which I will explain in a moment." He put his hands behind his back. "The *Nightblade* was indeed destroyed due to the actions of rogue elements within the Federation Navy. I survived using...experimental technology that I will not disclose at this time. I was rescued by my daughter and sister and we came right here to speak with you about the gravity of the situation."

The president nodded. "Admiral Rigsby briefed me on the situation and the betrayal he believes goes all the way to the top of Fleet Command. I requested, discreetly, that an investigation be opened into the matter."

Rachel's father's face went blank. "That was not wise, Mr. President."

The president frowned. "Why not."

"Because it will draw attention to you, no matter how discreet you are." His eyes took on a glazed expression and he looked up and to the right. Rachel remembered that look from years when she was a child and her father would get that same look in his eyes. When she asked him about it he would tell her he was talking to his work. It wasn't a lie, technically, but he hadn't been truthful about which work he was talking to. His eyes re-focused and he looked...startled. "That was Bridgette. The FIA headquarters just came under attack."

The president's face contorted in shock and he put a hand to his chest. "What? The FIA headquarters? Attack by who?"

"She says Federation Marines."

The president went back to his desk and commed his assistant. "Marie, put me through too Fleet Command, now."

"Of course, Mr. President. Just one...oh," a sound like blaster fire sounded in the background and the link closed. The door separating the oval office from the assistant's office exploded inward, following by the body of a Guard. Another lay outside on the floor. Several Shadow Watch Guards rushed to cover the president and took the brunt of the shrapnel.

"Get him out of here!" the captain of the Shadow Watch Guards contingent said. The cluster of Guards protecting the president moved him toward the door leading to the secret entrance into the Hague House. Laser fire came through the door and burnt into the floor plus the ceiling and hit a few of the Guards who had formed a human shield.

Rachel withdrew her blaster pistol. "Let's go," she said to Reynaldo and Maggie. A glance at her father revealed he had grabbed a coilgun rifle from a fallen Guard and was firing back through the doorway, though smoke from the explosion and perhaps a smoke grenade obscured the view. She stepped up, trying to find a target.

"Grenade," one of the Guards shouted.

Rachel drew upon the gravity magic inside her and caused the grenade to fly back out the way it had come. It exploded and shouts of pain sounded from the room beyond. She hoped she hadn't hurt the president's assistant with the ordinance, though she feared the woman was already dead or fatally wounded. She was distantly aware of the door behind her opening but an explosion behind her caused her to turn.

The gaggle of Guards leading the president out of the room blew backward as the room the secret passage fed into exploded. The president was now buried under a pile of combat-laden bodies.

"Shit," Rachel exclaimed. "Behind us!" she warned.

Reynaldo and Maggie turned and aimed toward the opening where the door had been. No one came through, at first, but moments later two creatures on four legs with upright bodies, pincers for hands and curved mandibles flanking their faces charged in. The first creature grabbed one of the Guards by the leg with one pincer and lifted him up in the air, then grabbed his neck with the other pincer. A crack sounded as the creature exerted its strength and the Guard's head was chopped off. Blood spurted everywhere.

Shit, Rachel thought. *These must be the Krai'kesh.* She fired a few shots at the first creature, which were absorbed by its hard carapace, but was distracted by the second creature leaping through the air and about to land on the president's huddle of Guards. For their part, the Guards were trying to fire at the Krai'kesh but their bullets bounced off its armor. Rachel again drew on her gravity magic and bound the Krai'kesh to the room behind it. The Krai'kesh jerked as if caught in a strong wind and blew straight backward. She did the same to the first Krai'kesh before it could strike any more of the Guards. She couldn't keep doing that, but it would give the Guards more time to take them down.

A glance behind her showed her father was still fighting the human foes coming from the main entrance. The smoke had cleared, revealing several opponents taking cover behind a desk and other furniture in the room beyond. They did not relent in their hurling of laser fire toward the defenders. *We're surrounded*, she thought.

"Rachel!" her father called. "Get ready to use your magic!"

My magic? Rachel thought. She was already using her gravity magic and her elemental magic was blocked by the nullification field. *Oh.*

Her father ducked down behind the president's desk and closed his eyes. Moments later Rachel felt a pressure lift from her brain as the nullification field was deactivated. *All right*, she thought before drawing on the elemental side of her magic. *Thanks, mom.* She had never met her mother, but the gift she had given her, elemental magic, lived on in her. She extended her mind and felt the air in the room where the human assailants lay. She felt the absence of life in the secretary and Shadow Watch Guards and felt no remorse forming a wall of flame and sending it careening into the room. The enemy took cover but the flame wall washed over the furniture like waves crashing against a rock. The enemies beyond caught on fire. The room she occupied became chillier than it had been before.

A shadowy mist formed against one wall of the oval office. It materialized into Bridgette. She wore full combat armor and wielded two pistols. Knives hung from a combat belt.

Of course, Rachel thought. *He disabled the nullification field so Bridgette could enter.*

Bridgette did not pay the human assailants, or what remained of them, any mind. She rushed toward the Krai'kesh, who even then were coming through the door again under a hail of coilgun fire, and leapt toward the first one. She disappeared into mist and a second later reappeared behind the creature. She fired her pistols into its head, causing it to scream in pain.

The monster swiped a pincer upward, trying to swat her off, but she faded to mist and re-appeared behind the second monster. She held knives this time, with the pistols now hanging from her combat belt. She stabbed upward and green fluid streamed down and passed through a cloud of mist as she again disappeared. She re-appeared in front of her now-bleeding target and fired point blank in its mouth before disappearing. Green blood spurted from its mouth and the creature toppled forward.

The second skittering monstrosity fell to a barrage of concentrated coilgun fire.

A roar echoed from the direction of the secret entrance. The sound of boots and shouts of anger sounded from the direction of the main entrance.

"We need to get him out of here," her father shouted over the din. "Bridgette, do your thing!"

"Everyone huddle up by the president," Bridgette barked. "Makes it easier."

Rachel and the others all came close to where the president was covered by his Guards. They each put a hand on the armor of a Guard.

"Here we go," Bridgette said. The world faded to gray as they shifted into the Shadow Realm.

Blink. They were outside the Hague House. *Blink.* They were outside back at Bard's Landing outside the *Renegade*. The world came back into color as they shifted back to reality. Rachel released a breath she didn't realize she had been holding.

The Guards huddled over the president rose and the president could stand at last. He stretched and looked around. "Where are we?"

"My ship," Rachel said, extending a hand toward the *Renegade*. The ramp was already lowering. "And our way out of here."

The president held up a hand. "Wait. I can't leave yet. There are traitors in the Hague House, the FIA headquarters has been attacked. The Federation needs its president."

"They need their president alive," Dawyn said. "We're outnumbered. Someone somewhere has planned this out in excruciating detail. If we hadn't been there to evacuate you..."

"I'd have been dead," the president finished.

"What I want to know is what the hell were those creatures?" Maggie asked.

"Devil-spawn," Reynaldo guessed.

"Krai'kesh," Rachel and her father said at once.

The president shook his head. "It is disturbing to see them here on Tar Ebon. I could understand Draxon II, but at the heart of the Federation?"

"Someone smuggled them in specifically for this attack," Rachel's father said. "As I said, this conspiracy goes deep. Likely right to the top."

"Then who can we trust?" the president asked.

"No one, until we know more." He turned to Bridgette. "What happened at FIA headquarters? You didn't tell me."

"I was gathering the documents relating to the Cult of Rae when alarms went off. Federation Marines, or least they were dressed like Marines, stormed the building. Our agents tried to fend them off but...we were betrayed from within." She shook her head. "I can't believe my own agents would turn on their brothers and sisters in uniform. I thought they were better than that."

Better than Marines and naval personnel, she means, Rachel thought.

"What happened next?"

"I grabbed the intel on the Cult of Rae, fought off some intruders and evacuated."

"I'm sorry for your loss."

Bridgette looked him in the eyes. "Don't be sorry. I'm not sorry. I'm angry. I'm ready to kick ass and take down the names of the traitors."

"We will get revenge, I promise."

"Where to next?" the president asked.

"We will rendezvous with the *Independence*. Do you know where they were last, Mr. President?"

"Yes. But so do the traitors, I fear."

"We just have to make one stop first and then we will go to them."

Chapter 14 - Dancing in the Moonlight

Kimberly, Baillidh and Corbin passed through the checkpoint to return to the wealthy part of town without issue. They arrived back at the Federation embassy and returned to their room.

"All right, so what's the plan?" Corbin asked.

"Well, we need to get Baillidh into the server room," Kimberly began. "Any ideas on how to do that?"

"Yes," Baillidh agreed. "I need to physically connect my datapad to the server to access it or use a transmitter to establish a secure connection."

Corbin pointed to a vent on the wall. "'Ow 'bout crawlin' through the vent?"

"Who's going to do the crawling," Kimberly asked. "You?"

"'Oi'm small enough, ain't oi? Or are ye callin' me fat?"

"Well, you *have* been drinking a lot," Kimberly noted.

Corbin stood up straighter and sucked in his stomach. "Well, oi can still suck in me gut, don't you worry."

"Now let's see if we can lift you up there," Baillidh said.

Kimberly looked at him and quirked an eyebrow. "Did you just make a joke, Baillidh?" He *never* made jokes.

Baillidh shrugged. "You two are rubbing off on me, I guess."

"Always with da fat jokes," Corbin grumbled.

"Wait," Baillidh held up a hand. "I have to give you a transmitter." He rummaged around in his backpack for several moments until his hand emerged clutching a small device. "Plug this into a socket on the server and I'll be able to tap in just as if I were plugged in directly."

Corbin took the transmitter and approached the wall beneath the vent. "Give me a boost, will ye?"

"Do you know where you're going?" Kimberly asked.

"Well, no, but oi figured ye would tell me when oi got there."

I guess the alcohol is still going to his head, Kimberly thought. "Baillidh, can you pull up a map?"

"Yeah, give me a second," he said, eyes glued to the datapad. A moment later a hologram projected out of the back of it. "We are here," he said, pointing to a blinking red dot inside a room near the top of the embassy. "The server room is here." A blinking blue dot appeared two floors below them on the other side of the building.

"At least oi'll be going downhill, otherwise oi'd need me climbin' gear." He cracked his knuckles and approached the wall. "Give me a lift, will ye?"

Kimberly put her hand beneath one foot and Baillidh beneath another and together they lifted Corbin up. He opened the vent and crawled inside. "'Ere I go."

His movement made a clanging sound at first, but it soon faded. "What's your status?" Kimberly asked several minutes later.

"Gettin' a little tight in 'here," Corbin reported. "But oi'm comin' up on the room now. Oi...dropping...in," static obscured his words.

"Corbin? Corbin?" Kimberly asked. She looked at Baillidh.

He shrugged. "Probably interference. It shouldn't interfere with my transmitter, though, as it's set on a different frequency."

"*If* Corbin succeeds. He could have been captured already for all we know."

A beep sounded from Baillidh's datapad. "Well, he hasn't been captured yet, ma'am. I'm getting a signal from the transmitter." He tapped on the datapad for several seconds. "I'm in. Downloading the files now. Corbin can come back."

"I don't have any way to reach him," Kimberly said. For a moment she considered shouting into the vents, but she knew he wouldn't hear her.

"Did ye get what ye need?" Corbin's voice came over the comm.

Kimberly breathed a sigh of relief. "Yes! You can come back now."

"Do oi leave the transmitter thingy behind?"

"Yes," Baillidh said. "It gives us a back door and it has a self-destruct mechanism if it's detected and removed."

"Aye, on me way back." He hesitated. "Eh, how do oi get back up them vents I slid down?"

"Baillidh, the map again please," Kimberly asked. "Hang tight, Corbin."

"Don' worry, lass. Oi ain't got nowhere to go."

She zoomed in and studied the rooms along the floor he was on, as well as below him. "I found a spot. Go three vents over and drop down. It's a broom closet."

"Oi always wanted ta come out o' the closet," he said. He kept his comm open as he shuffled through the vent. "Oof, tha' screw 'urt." At last came a "'ere we go," followed by a thud. "Made it," he said.

"Get back here ASAP," Kimberly ordered.

"Awe, oi was thinkin' abou' stoppin' ta flirt wit' the pretty girls. Oi guess oi'll put it off fer now."

Kimberly rolled her eyes.

Several minutes later he arrived. She suspected he had stopped to flirt with at least one girl, based on the silly grin on his face. "Thank you for joining us. Baillidh, show him what we've got."

"Well, we're no closer to finding out who the mole is, but we *do* know where the transmission went. It was text-based."

"And? Don't keep us in suspense," Kimberly demanded.

"Artois Industries," he said after another suspense-building moment.

"One of the merchant houses?" Kimberly asked, racking her brain.

"Aye. One o' the worst," Corbin said.

"The transmission mentions 'the cargo,' which I presume to mean the Krai'kesh," Baillidh noted.

Kimberly nodded. "We knew at least one merchant house was behind the Krai'kesh infiltration of Crossroad Station, but now we have proof it was House Artois." She paused. "Well, we have proof they were behind the attack on the resistance forces. But this file," she pointed to the datapad, "wouldn't contain any other information about how many Krai'kesh there are in our galaxy or where House Artois has been moving them, would it?"

"No, ma'am," Baillidh said. "Not unless they were transmitting that information to the mole, which would be highly unlikely."

"Well, it's something. But we need more."

"So wha's the next step?" Corbin asked.

"We infiltrate House Artois," Kimberly said.

"'Ow we gonna do tha'?"

Kimberly smiled. "By faking it till we make it."

KIMBERLY HELD HER HEAD high as she waited in line to enter the Artois estate. Women in elaborate dresses and men in stylish suits chatted, gossiped, and laughed all around her. She did not tug at her dress or do anything that would show her discomfort in the high heel shoes she wore. Why did she always end up wearing high heels when going undercover?

Corbin stood behind her and to her right, dressed in a dapper suit. He *did* pick at his suit. He also grumbled words under his voice.

"What are you doing?" Kimberly whispered, turning her head as little as possible to not draw attention.

"Gettin' inta character, m'lady. Remember, oi'm the bumblin' idiot servant."

"Well, you're being convincing. Keep it up." She turned her attention back to her surroundings. She cast her haughty gaze over the participants around her waiting in line, then swept her eyes across the rooftop and toward the estate grounds. Security was tight, with guards on the roof and scattered around the lawn. Guard towers occupied the corners of the large perimeter fence. *Is this a fortress or a house?* she wondered.

The line moved faster and she was soon passing through the security scanner. Part of the discomfort she struggled to suppress came from having to leave her pistol with Baillidh outside the perimeter. He assured her there was no way to smuggle the weapon in considering the advanced technology the security forces were using.

The guard swiped her identi-card and a moment later a beep sounded. He handed it back. "Welcome to the party, Madam Sommrich," a servant dressed like Corbin said from beyond the scanner. He bowed from the waist and extended an arm straight out, fingers pointing toward the interior of the building.

Kimberly gave a regal sniff and passed through. Corbin went through security without incident, though the servant who welcomed Kimberly was silent as he passed and fell into position behind her as they entered a lavish hallway. A red runner covered the tile floor and directed their path. Old-fashioned wall sconces, though filled with modern lighting orbs, gave a sense of a medieval castle. The hallway opened into an enormous ballroom. Chandeliers with actual candles hung from the ceiling, a grand staircase led to the second floor at the back of the room and hundreds of people danced in the center or stood and sat along the sides.

Corbin let out a whistle, which prompted a glare from Kimberly. "Wha'? Da drunk servant can't be in awe?"

"You're supposed to be used to it," Kimberly whispered. "I'm rich, remember?" She had to admit she was impressed by the grandeur of the ballroom. Such old-style eloquence from an age long past was rare in the Federation, replaced by functional buildings designed more for space savings than for style.

"An' oi'm drunk and can barely stand," he said, purposely stepping forward and staggering.

Kimberly slapped him on the back of the head, partly to remain in character as a rich merchant dealing with a presumptuous servant who dared to walk ahead of her and partly because of genuine annoyance with him.

I'm in, she said through her implant. *How do I get to the server room here?*

I don't know, ma'am, Baillidh said. If he were communicating via voice she imagined he would sound remorseful.

Then how the hell am I supposed to find out?

Ye could ask someone, Corbin said.

Yes but... she trailed off as her eyes focused on a man wearing a military dress uniform and surrounded by a gaggle of hangers-on. Facial recognition from her implant identified the man as Frederick Artois, a high-ranking family member and officer within House Artois. *I think I found a way.*

She walked toward the man but she had no sooner made it halfway there than she heard a voice calling out to her from behind. "Miss Sommrich, is that you?"

Kimberly turned, masking her annoyance. She knew that voice. "Ambassador Barrius, there you are." She offered a curtsy. "I apologize for not recognizing you sooner."

The ambassador puffed up his chest. "Not to worry, my fair maiden." He extended a hand. "May I have this dance?" He did not look her in the eyes, instead preferring to stare at her bosom.

Kimberly wanted to slap him or, better yet, shoot him, but she kept her composure and placed her hand in his. "It would be my pleasure." She gave Corbin a dirty look when she saw the huge grin on his face as she was led to the center of the dance floor. She didn't have time for distractions like this, but didn't have a choice.

The ambassador led and she followed. He tried to twirl her but failed miserably as she spun and almost fell. When he leaned in for a kiss she turned her face away and pushed him back. "Now now, Ambassador. Let us not be so familiar," she said in her best haughty voice.

The ambassador, rather than being offended by her rejection, smiled like a jackal eying some prey it was chasing. "Of course, m'lady." His eyes again strayed across her body starting at her toes and briefly meeting her eyes before again settling on her chest. He was a pig.

Seeing an opportunity, Kimberly slapped him in the face. She raised her voice. "You do me a great disrespect, sir. I shall find another partner." She stormed off but made sure her path took her past Frederick Artois. She put her face in her hands as she passed and made sobbing noises. Out of the corner of her eye she caught him watching her. *Please follow me*, she thought. Princes, or rich merchant children who fancied themselves as royalty anyway, could not resist the pull of a damsel in distress and Frederick was no different. She sat down at a table and put her head in her hands. *Stay where you are, Corbin*, she said through the implant. *I'm trying to lure Frederick in.*

It's workin' m'lady. E's headin' over.

"Are you all right, m'lady?" a higher pitched male voice asked. "Did that man hurt you?" A chair scraped on the floor.

She raised her head and it was indeed Frederick Artois sitting there watching her. She wiped a tear from her eye and shook her head, looking in the direction of the ambassador. "No, he's just a lecherous pig." She smiled at Frederick. "My name is Evonne. What is yours?"

"Frederick," he said, sitting up a little straighter. "Would you like me to have him removed from the premises?"

Kimberly shook her head. "No, no, let him be. He's an ambassador from Tar Ebon, you know."

Frederick made a spitting motion. "Pfft, the Federation. Bunch of do-gooders who fancy themselves the police of the galaxy."

She smiled. "*I* am from Tar Ebon."

His face went slack. "Well, other than you, of course. You are radiant."

Kimberly averted her eyes and pretended to bashful. "You're too kind."

"Are you a politician?" he asked.

She put a hand to her chest. "Heavens no! Could I afford this if I were a politician?" She put a hand on her necklace. "I am a merchant. Sommrich Industries."

"Hmmm, never heard of it," he said, scratching his beard.

She met his eyes, a plan to distract him from pondering the identity of her fake business forming in her mind. "Is there some place more...private we can go?" She raised her eyebrows to emphasize what she was suggesting they do in a private place.

"Of...of course," he stammered, rising to his feet and offering a hand. "Right this way, m'lady. I know just the place."

She took his hand and rose to her feet. *Try to find a way out of the ballroom, Corbin*, she ordered. *I'm going to try to get what I can out of this guy.*

Jus' don't get too cozy wit' 'im, Corbin said.

Oh shut up, she said and shut down the link.

He led her up the grand staircase down a hallway deeper into the palace. "Do you like my home?" he asked as they walked.

"It is very impressive," she said as they turned a corner. "Have you lived here all your life?"

"Oh yes, I was born here," he said. "It's our ancestral home. I used to race down these halls with my sister." He led her around another corner.

"Is your sister home?" she asked, trying to make small talk.

"In a way. She came home but my father imprisoned her."

"For what?"

"Dishonoring the family, fighting for the Federation, that sort of thing."

"She fought for the Federation?"

"Yeah, she was a pilot."

A Federation pilot, here? Imprisoned? "Oh." She decided to change the subject. "Where are we going?" she asked.

"To my quarters," he said. A door stood at the end of the hallway, a pair of guards flanking it. They saluted as he passed and opened the door. He held it for her and she nodded her thanks and entered.

High vaulted ceilings gave the room a cavernous feel. A massive four-poster bed was centered on the wall opposite the door. A wall of glass occupied the area to the right. She could not see what it overlooked.

Frederick caught her eying the window and explained. "The palace was originally built overlooking a lake."

Kimberly stepped up to the window and looked out. While she could see where a lake might have been, all she saw now was factories and warehouses. "Where did the lake go?"

"It was emptied during development of the area." He locked the door to his room.

"Oh, how sad," she said.

He shrugged. "It was necessary. Besides, it allows me to survey my father's assets."

"Of course. It's a beautiful view," she replied.

"Now that we're somewhere private..." He came up behind her and wrapped his arms around her. "What did you want to do?"

Why does every man on this damn planet want to put their hands on me? She wondered. She grabbed his hands and jerked his arms up, then spun and kneed him in the groin. He grunted in shock and then groaned in pain. "What..." he began.

She punched him in the face, then covered his mouth and pushed him onto the bed. She set her clutch on the nightstand, straddled him, and grabbed him in the groin and squeezed. "Now listen to me, you little creep. I need information and you're going to give it to me or you'll become a damn eunuch." She wasn't sure how she would accomplish that without a knife or blade but fortunately she didn't need to.

His eyes went wide and he wheezed out a "Please...don't."

"Then are you going to answer my questions?"

He nodded vigorously.

"Where are the servers in this place?"

"The basement," he wheezed, which brought on a fit of coughing.

"Is there a code required to access them?"

"Five, nine, three, seven, one," he said.

"Excellent, thank you. Have a nice nap." Before he could respond she took his head and slammed it against one of the posts until he was unconscious. She then ruffled her hair to make it look messy, kissed the sheets to smear her lipstick and pulled one part of her dress down so it was uneven with the other side. She grabbed her clutch and went to the door, unlocked it and stepped outside. "He's sleeping," she said, not looking at the guards.

The guards said nothing in response to her statement and did not look in the room to verify. *They must see this all the time*, she thought as she walked down the hall. She resisted the urge to look back, as that could imply guilt. No, she had just been there for a good shag and now she was off.

The server is in the basement, Baillidh, she said through her implant. *Corbin, where are you?*

Oi'm hidin' in da supply closet.

Another closet? Seriously?

Aye.

Why?

Oi may have stolen a chicken from the kitchen. The chef chased me with a damn butcher knife. Twas the only place oi could hide.

Well is it safe to come out now?

Le' me look. A moment passed. *Looks like the coast is clear. Where am oi meetin' ye?*

Find a way down to the basement. Maybe there's a servant staircase or something?

Oi'll check it out. 'Ow are you gettin' down there?

An elevator lay at the end of the hall. *Elevator.* She approached and pressed the call button. The doors opened immediately and she stepped inside. She hit the basement button and the elevator descended two floors to the basement. Time was critical, as she didn't know how long Frederick would remain unconscious or undisturbed. All it would take would be a servant or more curious guard to enter and see him beaten up to sound the alarm. She brushed her hair with her hand, trying to bring it back into order and straightened her dress. She opened her clutch, withdrew a tube of lipstick and re-applied it.

The doors opened and she stepped out, looking both ways. She saw no one, but was at a crossroad. *Baillidh, still no luck on getting schematics?*

No, nothing. You're on your own, sorry.

"Well this way is ruled out," Corbin said, strolling down the center hallway. He tilted his head to indicate the path behind him. "Da kitchens be tha' way."

"That leaves us with two." No signage indicated the proper path. "Let's split up," she said. "You go that way, I'll go this way." She pointed to the right. "If you find the server room, plug your transmitter in."

"And if oi dun find the server room?"

"Then head back this way because it means I *did* find it."

"Righto, lass. Good luck to ye."

The two split up. Kimberly sneaked down the hallway, straining to hear any sounds ahead. The hallway curved, so it was impossible to see what lay ahead. A sound made her stop. Someone talking. She crept up and peaked around the bend.

A man sat at a metal desk, his feet propped up. Another man sat at a table with a deck of playing cards. He was playing cards alone. "No, listen, that's not how it happened. See..."

Kimberly tuned them out and focused on what lay behind them. A sign that read "Prison Area: Authorized Personnel Only." *This must be the prison Frederick mentioned before. The one his sister is imprisoned in, right?* Kimberly considered turning around and going back the other way. Obviously Corbin would be the one to reach the servers if she'd run into the prison block. But something tugged at her. A sense of duty? Perhaps. Frederick's sister was an Artois, true, but she was also a Federation pilot, a fact which had landed her in prison in the first place. Kimberly owed it to her to at least attempt a rescue. *Corbin, did you find the server room?*

Aye, he responded. *Oi found it. Oi'm pluggin in this dongle now fer Baillidh. What did ye find?*

A prison block. There's a Federation pilot being held captive there.

Le' me guess. Ye want ta rescue 'er?

You got it.

She imagined him sighing in frustration. *And ye got yer mind made up do ye?*

Yes.

Fine. 'Ang tight, oi'm on me way.

Please hurry, she thought. While she waited she checked up on Baillidh. *Have you hacked their servers, Baillidh?*

I'm in. Found lots of juicy data, ma'am. I'm saving it all and packaging it up to transmit to FIA headquarters as soon as we get a chance. But ma'am, it's worse than we thought.

The Krai'kesh proliferation?

Yes. It seems they have sleeper cells throughout the Federation. House Artois has been using their existing trade routes to secretly transport clusters of Krai'kesh to strategic planets and locations.

Damn it. Is there any insight as to how the Krai'kesh entered our galaxy without us knowing before now?

Your guess is as good as mine, ma'am. There's nothing speaking to their origins.

All right, a mystery for another day. Corbin is here. Gotta go.

Corbin sauntered up but was breathing heavy.

"Did you run?" Kimberly asked.

"Oi may 'ave sprinted. Fer a little ways."

Kimberly almost laughed but caught herself. That might catch the attention of the Guards. Instead she whispered. "I've never seen you run."

"And ye probably never will," Corbin said.

Kimberly peaked around the corner again. The guards hadn't moved from their spots. She and Corbin had no weapons. How were they going to take on two guards She eyed Corbin. "I have an idea," she whispered.

Moments later she staggered around the corner and made her way down the corridor toward the guards. She bobbed her head to the side and then rolled it back, mouth open, before letting it hang as she swerved all around. Corbin followed a moment later.

"Mistress, please come back!" he pleaded. "Ye've had to much ta drink."

"No, I... haven't," she slurred, continuing toward the guards, who had risen from their seats.

The guard who had his feet up moments earlier held up a hand. "What's going on here?"

"It's me mistress," Corbin said. "She drank too much, stumbled down here. Oi've been lookin' all over fer her."

Kimberly reached the guard standing by the table and staggered into him. He caught her and she looked up into his face. "My hero," she said. Then she leaned her head back so she was looking at Corbin upside down.

Corbin raced up by her side and neared the guard by the desk. "If ye can just tell us where da elevator be we'll be on our way."

The guard cleared his throat. He was watching Kimberly with a hungry look in his eyes. Could he see down her dress from that angle? "Well you just...oof," he doubled over as Corbin grabbed him by the shirt and punched him in the face. Then he climbed on the desk and rode him down to the floor.

Kimberly took advantage of the moment to punch the guard holding her in the groin. He let go of her but she stayed on her feet. He doubled over in pain. She took advantage and kneed him in the face. He fell backward, unconscious. "Hurry, find the controls for that door," she said as she straightened her dress and ran her hands through her hair.

"Got it," Corbin said, pressing several buttons on the console. The security door beeped for a few seconds before sliding open. "And oi got the keycard." He held up a lanyard.

"Do we have anything to tie these two up with?"

"Le' me see." He opened a drawer and rummaged through it. Seconds later he withdrew two pairs of stun cuffs. "These will work." He placed them on the wrists of both men.

Kimberly led the way into the prison. She braced herself in case another guard was on duty inside, but she saw no guards. Instead, at the end of the row of cells she found a woman dressed in a Federation Navy uniform.

The woman, who must be Selene, eyed them dubiously from where she stood against the far wall of her cell. "Who are you?"

Kimberly pointed to herself. "Hello, Selene. My name is Kimberly Hague. I'm an FIA operative. This is Corbin. He's also an agent."

"'Ello," Corbin said, bowing. "Aren't ye a pretty lass?"

She stepped toward the entrance of her cell. "Seriously? This isn't some test or cruel joke? My father didn't send you?"

"I haven't met your father, though if your brother is any indication, I probably don't want to."

The woman breathed a sigh of relief. "My father is much worse than my brother. You're lucky you *haven't* met him yet. Are you here to get me out?"

"Well, we didn't know you were in here until your brother let it slip during conversation. But of course, we'll get you out. Corbin, would you do the honors?"

Corbin removed the lanyard with the keycard and pressed it to the security console. A beep sounded and the force field blocking her door deactivated.

Selene walked out. "Thank you. I was going to be executed soon."

"Executed. Your own father was going to have you executed?" Kimberly couldn't believe it.

"As I said, my father is far worse than my brother."

"Well, let's head upstairs and then we can..."

An alarm sounded and a voice came over the speakers in the prison area. "Intruders in the building. I repeat, intruders in the building. Implement lockdown procedures."

"Shit," Kimberly said. "Frederick woke up."

"Woke up? What did you do to him?" Selene asked.

Kimberly sighed. "I seduced him. He took me up to his room, I beat him up, got information out of him, and knocked him out. I guess I thought he would stay down a little longer."

Selene covered her mouth and laughed. "I'm sorry, I don't mean to laugh. But that is hilarious." She adopted a more serious expression. "So what are we going to do?"

"They don't know where we are or they wouldn't have sounded a general alarm and implemented a lockdown. So let's see if we can sneak out." Kimberly led them toward the door of the prison.

No sooner had they exited the prison than four guards came around the bend. The lead guard took in the scene with two guards incapacitated on the floor and activated his comm. "Intruders in the prison area. I repeat, intruders in the prison area."

"Get back," Kimberly warned, shoving Selene and Corbin back into the prison. She slapped the control to shut the door just as blaster bolts slammed into the walls around the door. "Corbin, can that keycard lock down the console?"

"Oi'll try." Corbin stepped up to the console and pulled up a menu. He chose the lock option and when prompted held the keycard up to it. The screen flashed red and indicated the door was locked. "Dunno how long that'll hold em," he said.

Now to figure out a way to escape, Kimberly thought.

Chapter 15 - Attempted Rescue

"Ah, Epsilon III," John said, leaning back in his chair as the auto-pilot led the *Dauntless* toward the surface. "It's been what, two hundred years?"

"I forget," Ashley said. "You told Selene once."

"Any idea where she and Emma are being held?" Derek asked.

"Well, the obvious choice would be the Artois palace."

"They have a palace?"

"All the merchants and large corporations do. House Artois is both. Artois Industries *and* House Artois. They're one of the titans of industry."

"Which means we're going to have to fight our way in," Ethan said.

"Yes, Mr. Marine, we're going to have to fight our way in. Most likely."

"*Or* we could, you know, try a diplomatic solution," Ashley said.

None of the men said anything.

Ashley sighed. "Boys and their guns."

They entered the atmosphere and flew toward the landing zone. It was conveniently located on the other side of the House Artois palace they suspected Selene and Emma were being held in. They passed over a desolate landscape dotted with small towns and huge factories. "What is this place?" Derek asked.

"The Dark Zone," Ashley explained. "The Commerce Sector isn't known for their human rights or social services. The Dark Zone is where the poor and lower middle-class people live in what amounts to feudal serfdom."

"It's a sore subject with her," John commented.

"Why does the Federation allow it?" Derek asked.

"Son, we learned a long time ago not to try to fix the world."

"Most of us," Ashley grumbled.

John motioned toward Ashley with his head. "Except for social justice warriors like my wife. She *tried* to bring about a revolution years ago when the merchant families were still on Tar Ebon. No dice. The movements were shut down quick and Ashley almost found herself six feet under."

"It would have worked if the senate had backed us," Ashley protested.

"Whatever you say, honey cake."

Ethan made a gagging noise.

"As I was saying, the merchants tolerated no usurping of the social pecking order. It got worse when they got their own section of the galaxy to rule over. The Federation had bigger fish to fry and couldn't afford to get into a war with the Commerce Sector, so we let it go.

Ashley sniffed.

They passed over the wall separating the Dark Zone from the brightly lit main city. The *Dauntless* rose as it flew over skyscrapers. On the far side of the city, with a backdrop of Dark Zone factories, sat a sprawling palace lit up bright. Derek noticed something strange as they came closer. "Uh, guys, there's a ton of police or security force presence here."

"Yeah, I see it," John said. "Do you think jailbreak?"

"Wouldn't surprise me," Ashley said. "Emma hates being locked up."

"Well, let's take a detour and find out." John took control back from the auto-pilot and dipped lower, preparing to land near the palace.

A beep sounded from the comm. John answered it. "Attention starship *Dauntless*, this is Epsilon Flight Control. You have deviated from your course. You will return to your flight path or we will be forced to take action against you."

John muted the comm. "Dang, that's a quick response time to a deviation," John said. "Might be a record."

"Unless someone is watching us," Ethan said.

John formed a thumbs up and pointed it toward Ethan. "Good thinking. Well, I've always been a rebel. Let's do this." He un-muted the comm. "Epsilon Flight Control, we have a date with the head of House Artois. Do what you have to do." He clicked off the comm before they could respond.

"John, we're not on Federation soil here," Ashley warned. "If we get captured there's very little political recourse for us."

"I know, babe. Plus the in-depth rectal exams scare me and I don't look good in orange." He reached over and patted her arm. "It'll be okay."

Derek rolled his eyes and smiled but it disappeared as his thoughts drifted to Selene. *We're coming, Selene. Hang on.*

The *Dauntless* landed on the roof of the palace because, as John put it, "why not." The four of them stood up. A beep from the comm stopped them. John hit the comm again. "Listen, Flight Control, you can go screw yourselves."

"This is not Flight Control," a male voice said quickly.

"Then who are you?" John asked.

"My name is Baillidh. I am an FIA operative."

"FIA. That's awfully convenient. How did you know we were on planet?"

"Because I am watching you right now from outside the perimeter and picked up your transmitter ID."

"What are you doing outside the perimeter?"

"Two of my fellow agents are inside the building. In fact, they're trapped in the dungeons below the palace."

"So *that's* what all the security presence is for."

"Excuse me, Baillidh," Derek interjected. "We're looking for two Federation Navy pilots. Emma Edgerton and Selene Artois. Do you know anything about them? Have you heard their names?"

"I know the second name. Two fellow agents are stuck in the dungeons with her. The first name though, I recognize it from history books but she's not with them as far as I know."

Ethan punched the back of John's chair. "Damn it."

John raised his hand to call for calm. "Okay, Baillidh. We're on our way down. Can you send us whatever you have on the schematics of this place or whatever so we can get there fast?"

"Yes, sending my intel over now." Data began to stream over. "There are blueprints and everything we know about House Artois' dealings with the Krai'kesh."

"Wonderful," John said. "If they're working with the Krai'kesh I won't feel so bad nailing them to the wall. Figuratively."

"I will literally nail every member of the Artois family to a wall if they've harmed Emma," Ethan said.

"Except Selene," Derek said.

"Of course."

"We'll be in touch, Baillidh. *Dauntless* out." John closed the link. The group of four and Ethan's Marines geared up and exited the ship. "Ethan, leave one of your men behind, to guard the ship," John said. "This place is probably crawling with mercenaries who would just love to steal this old girl."

Nice, Derek thought.

Ethan assigned one of his Marines to remain aboard and then the group set off toward a stairwell. Security vehicles appeared on the horizon, heading toward the palace.

John paused halfway. "Wait, I'm going to give it some extra protection." He closed his eyes and the *Dauntless* blurred and disappeared. He re-opened his eyes. "There, they won't be able to see it."

They encountered no resistance as they descended the stairwell to one floor below the roof. They exited and made their way to the elevator, but on the way four security guards rounded the corner. They stopped and shouted, "intruders on level four," before drawing their laser pistols and firing in the direction of John and the others. The security officers were inundated with laser fire in return and quickly neutralized.

The group continued to the service elevator but it was shut down. "This is cozy," John said. "Uh, Baillidh, can you restart the elevator?"

"Give me a second," Baillidh said.

Derek heard shouting coming from the stairwell down the hall. "We've got company," he pointed out.

The elevator jerked and descended. "That's what I'm talkin' about," John said. The elevator stopped. "Ugh, what's going on, Baillidh old buddy?"

"The emergency safeguards reasserted themselves. I'm trying to override them."

Elevator music started playing from the speaker on the wall. "Really?" John asked. He banged his head against the wall. "You just had to turn on the music."

"Sorry," Baillidh said. The music turned off. "I'm trying to..." he said as the elevator jerked. "There we go." It continued its downward descent.

"Remind me to buy you a drink when this is all over, B."

"If we survive this," Ashley said.

"You're supposed to leave the pessimism to your son."

"Where do you think he gets it?" she asked.

"Good point."

The elevator stopped at the basement level and the doors creaked open. John strode out but was forced to leap back as laser fire flashed in front of him.

Ethan shoved his father aside and rolled out, coming up on one knee and firing to the left. Other Marines ran out and started firing in either direction. Derek leaned around the corner and fired to the right, where security forces were just turning around. Something had them pre-occupied. "I think the prison is that way," he said, pointing.

"Lieutenant, escort my parents to the prison," Ethan said. "My men and I will hold off the enemy."

"Yes, sir," Derek said. He looked over at Ashley and John. "You two ready?"

"You know it."

Derek came around the corner and fired straight at the security forces. A beam of light flashed toward him but slammed into a wall of light. All the beams of light did as John absorbed the energy from them. A fireball hurtled toward the enemy and exploded in their midst, sending several running away, their armor on fire.

They rounded the corner and found a group of guards aiming at a closed blast door while one man used a blow torch on the door. The door glowed orange as it heated up. They were almost through the door.

John whistled. "Hey, boys, over here!" he shouted.

The group of guards turned and fired toward him. His shield of light held and the beams disappeared. John began to glow with a white light. One of the guards threw a flashbang. Derek activated the sound and light dampeners on his helmet and shouted, "Flash bang."

Ashley and John covered their ears and closed their eyes. The grenade went off but instead of flashing at the trio it streamed toward John. "That was a mistake," John said, though Derek doubted the enemy could hear him. He interlaced his fingers and cracked them. He extended his arms to the side and a curtain of visible light formed, covering the corridor from ceiling to floor. He made a pushing motion and the curtain flashed forward.

The enemy forces were incinerated before they could scream. Only dust remained on the floor.

John dusted his hands. "Damn I'm good. That's like what, two incinerations in a week?"

"Let me get a pin to pop that ego of yours," Ashley said. "I wouldn't want you to float away."

The torch used to cut through the door lay on the ground, deactivated when its owner died.

The trio approached the door. "Hello in there," John shouted. "You alive?"

"John, is that you?" Selene's voice came through the thick blast door.

"Yep. Ashley, me, and your boyfriend at your service."

"Thank God."

"You gonna open the door and come out?"

"We can't. The door is stuck."

"Leave it to me," Ashley said, stepping up to it. She lifted the torch and turned it on. The flames started out normal size but moments later expanded and swirled around Ashley's arm. She touched her hand to the door and the entire center, which the original owner of the torch had been cutting out, melted to slag. She then touched the molten metal and Derek felt a wave of heat wash over him through his armor as she cooled the metal.

Selene stepped out first, followed by two other people Derek did not recognize. *These must be the FIA agents,* he thought. His eyes went back to Selene and remained locked there. He stepped forward and embraced and kissed her. "Derek," she said. "I missed you so much."

"I missed you too," Derek said.

Selene stepped back. "I have so much to tell you."

"Start by telling us where Emma is," Ashley said.

"We don't have time for this," the woman behind Selene said. "We should get out of here."

"Who are you?" John asked.

"I'm Kimberly Hague, FIA operative and team leader."

"And you, little dwarf man?" John said.

"The name's Corbin," he said.

John nodded to them each in turn. "It's a pleasure to meet you both. Shall we get to my ship?"

"You didn't tell us who *you* are."

"Selene didn't fill you in?"

"Der wasn't a whole lotta time ta talk, and Selene wasn't expectin' ye," Corbin said.

John put a hand on his chest. "I am John Edgerton. This is my lovely wife Ashley and this upstanding gentleman is Derek Jamison, the boyfriend of Selene."

"Wait, ye got a *boyfriend*?" Corbin asked Selene.

Selene smiled up at Derek. "Yes, I'm taken, Corbin."

"Awe darn it. Why do all da good ones be taken?"

"I'm not taken," Kimberly said.

"Eh, yer me boss," Corbin said, waving at her.

Kimberly shook her head and smirked. Her expression became serious. "Now that everyone has been introduced, can we please get out of here?"

"Sure. Right this way," John extended a hand back the way they'd come.

Ashley remained where she was, arms crossed and looking at Selene. Derek thought she looked like she was pleading with her eyes.

Selene took a deep breath. "Emma was taken by the Krai'kesh back when we were first captured. I don't know where they took her. I tried to go with her but they didn't want me. I'm sorry."

Ashley nodded, but Derek noticed her eyes were moister than usual before she turned to follow John.

The group arrived back at the intersection to find Ethan and his Marines no longer under attack. Ethan turned. "Right on time. We just beat back that wave, but I expect more will be on their way soon. The elevator just went crashing down, so I expect they cut the cable."

"Damn," John said. "So we have to fight our way out?"

"Looks that way."

"Wait," Selene said. "There's a secret passage that leads out of the palace to the woods outside the perimeter. It's closed up by rock but," she looked at Ashley, "you should have no trouble breaking through."

Ashley nodded. "Let's do it."

"Only one problem," John said. "The ship is on the roof."

"My Marine can fly it," Ethan said.

John shot him a glare. "I'm not trusting my baby to some random Marine."

"He has flight training."

"I don't care if he's the best pilot in the galaxy, he ain't flying the *Dauntless* and that's final."

Ethan sighed. "Fine. Can he at least activate the auto-pilot?"

John stroked his chin. "I suppose he can't mess *that* up."

"It's settled," Selene said, heading down the center hallway. "Follow me." She led the group past an elevator and stairwell. "That leads to the kitchens," she explained. Distant shouts came from behind the group, but no lasers flashed toward them. At the end of the hallway stood a blast door. Selene punched in a code at the control panel. The door slid open. "My brother and I used to play down here. This is the entrance to the catacombs."

"Your ancestors built catacombs?" John asked.

"When they first arrived here from Tar Ebon, yes."

"That's...archaic."

"It's the Commerce Sector," Ashley said dryly. "Their society is behind by several hundred years."

"Still. *Catacombs.*" John shook his head in disbelief.

"We could use some light," Selene said. "It's dark down there."

"Of course it is. Probably damp, too, right?"

Selene arched an eyebrow at him. "Are you scared of catacombs?"

John stood up straighter. "Not exactly. I just had a terrible experience with catacombs once, that's all. I thought my days exploring such places were behind me." He obliged by summoning a bright orb of light. He cast it forward through the door. It revealed a stone staircase that spiraled down. "Pretty narrow stairs."

"Hug the wall," Selene said, leading them.

The stairs twisted several times before they reached the bottom. The orb of light followed them. Derek felt dizzy. A massive statue stood in front of them, while rows of stone caskets lined the walls. "Who is that?" Derek asked, pointing at the statue.

"My great, great something grandfather, Vortimor Artois. He was the founder of House Artois in this sector.

"Great name," John said. "Not."

Selene, with the orb of light floating above her head, led them around the statue of Vortimor and straight down the center of the catacomb. Branches led to other rooms and hallways but she knew where she was going. They ended at a large boulder. "This is it. The entrance was sealed after I...well," she glanced at Derek and blushed. "Never mind. Can you open it, Ashley?"

Derek smirked, wondering what her secret was. He would have to ask her in private...if they got out of there alive. They still had to escape orbit.

"Stand back," Ashley commanded. She stepped forward and put her hand on the boulder. Derek could not see her eyes but imagined them glowing white. For several moments nothing happened, but then the boulder melted into the ground like a wax candle submerged in a forge fire. Ashley extended her arm toward the fresh opening and bowed. "My husband is not the only one who can do impressive things today." She flashed a triumphant smile at John.

John rolled his eyes. "I didn't know it was a competition."

"It's not, because I'll always win."

Shouts echoed through the catacombs. "We've got company," Ethan said. "Let's hurry unless you want us blowing up the catacombs."

"Everyone get inside, then I'll seal the entrance again," Ashley said. As the last Marine entered the tunnel she raised her arms and rock flowed up from the ground solidified, reforming the boulder. She dusted her hands. "Twice in one day."

John sniffed.

Selene and the orb of light led the way down the tunnel. It was not straight but did not have side tunnels to get lost down. It started going uphill. "We're almost out," she said. They arrived at a rust-covered door with a lock on the inside. Three steps led to it. Selene motioned. "Would one of you boys kindly break the lock?"

Derek walked up the steps, raised his rifle and broke the lock with the butt of it. He pulled the door open. Dirt streamed down and caused him to retreat to the side.

Selene led the way up the steps.

"Is this a tree?" Derek asked.

"Yes," Selene said. She pushed at one part of the tree and a panel popped out. "Pretty clever, right?"

"I'm impressed," he said.

"I'm letting Baillidh know where we are," Kimberly said as she emerged from the tree.

"Ethan, let your Marine know where we are too," John said, stretching. "All he has to do is punch in our coordinates and activate the auto-pilot. The old girl will take care of the rest."

Ethan nodded. "On it."

"Tell your guy to hurry," John said to Kimberly. "Once the *Dauntless* lands we'll be telling the security forces right where we are. They'll be swarming the forest."

"He's two minutes away and running as fast as he can," Kimberly said.

The palace towered in the distance within the perimeter fence. Security vehicles hovered over it like flies above feces. Some landed while others rose. Moments later an object rose from the top of the palace and headed their way. It had to be the *Dauntless*.

Security forces gave chase, firing at the *Dauntless*. *I guess John's invisibility field doesn't move with the ship.*

A rustling in the brush caused Derek to swing his rifle around and aim at a man emerging. The man held up his hands. "Woah, don't shoot," he said.

"Stand down," Kimberly ordered. "That's Baillidh."

Derek lowered his rifle. *Who does she think she is ordering me around?*

"Just in time, buddy," John said. He formed a fist and pointed it toward him.

Baillidh stared at the proffered fist.

"Come on," John urged. "Pound it."

Baillidh formed a fist and timidly pressed it against John's.

"There we go!"

"Here comes the *Dauntless*," Ethan announced.

The ship landed in a small field to the south of the group. They ran toward the extended ramp.

"They're closing on us!" Ethan shouted again.

Laser fire burned the ground around the group. One Marine went flying forward and landed on his stomach, smoking rising from his back. He turned over and writhed in pain.

John stopped and turned. The next barrage of lasers met another wall of light. "I can't hold them that long!" he shouted. "It's not like small arms fire." He waited until everyone, even the injured Marine, were aboard before running toward the *Dauntless*. He ran up the ramp just as the barrier evaporated. "Go, go!" he shouted, running for the cockpit. Derek followed, while Selene followed Kimberly and her team toward the back of the ship.

"You're the captain," Ashley said as the two men entered.

"Oh, right," John said, breathing heavy as he slumped into his chair and took a deep breath. "All right, let's do this." He activated the repulsors and the ship rose. Then he pulled back on a lever and it accelerated so fast Derek was pressed back into his seat despite the inertial dampeners.

"We've probably got half the planet on our tails by now," Ethan said. "Any bright ideas?"

"Fly until we're able to shift," John said.

"We're all going to die," Ethan replied.

"I have a better idea," Kimberly said from the doorway.

Where did she come from? Derek wondered.

"Okay, dear, what's your idea?" John asked as he jerked the ship to avoid a barrage from a pursuing vessel.

"I've contacted Isabelle. She's on her way."

"Isabelle?" Ashley said. "As in our niece Isabelle?"

"Yes."

"How do you know her?" John asked.

"I know her from Galatia IV," Kimberly explained.

"Ahh, nasty business, that."

"Yeah," Kimberly said but didn't elaborate.

"What's her ETA?"

"She didn't say. How fast can she move through shadow space?"

"Depends on where she started from."

"She was at Crossroad Station last I knew."

"Then she should be here any minute now," John said. The ship jerked sharply to the side and Kimberly almost crashed into a console. "You might want to go back and buckle in, darlin'."

"Good idea," Kimberly said. She turned and went back further in the ship.

The *Dauntless* climbed toward space, several security ships in hot pursuit. The sensor display showed more ships closing from the flanks and from in front of them. They were about to be surrounded. Derek opened his mouth to warn John of that when a gust of wind caused him to turn around.

A cloud of shadow and mist formed and materialized into a woman clad in armor and with short black hair. *That must be Isabelle*, Derek thought.

She looked around, her gaze taking in her surroundings. "I heard you needed a ride," she said.

John shrugged. "Yeah, we're surrounded and could use an emergency shift right about now."

"Any particular destination?"

"Anywhere but here, for now. Then we have to figure out where the Krai'kesh fleet that took Emma went."

"Wait, the Krai'kesh took Emma?"

"Yeah, out near the outer rim. We're going to get her back, though," John promised. "But we could really use a shift right about now." He pointed to the main display which mirrored the sensor console output.

"Shifting to Crossroad Station for now," Isabelle said. She closed her eyes and the world turned to gray as they entered shadow space.

THE *Dauntless* re-entered real-space a brief time later. Crossroad Station lay in the distance, two clusters of ships floating at opposite ends. "What's going on here?" John asked.

"Krai'kesh invasion of Crossroad Station complicated by an Imperial 'rescue' operation that is a thinly veiled takeover attempt. I've been here negotiating."

"'Negotiating' as in cracking skulls?"

"No. Glaring menacingly. Cracking skulls comes later. I'm going to debrief my agents. How are you going to find Emma?"

"I'm going to comm Admiral Rigsby," John said. "He should know where the Krai'kesh fleet is. Then we go crack Krai'kesh skulls. Literally."

"Count me in."

Chapter 16 - Fighting Back

"Admiral, we have a communication incoming from the *Dauntless*," Zigana reported.

"Put them through," Martin said from his captain's chair.

The vid screen displayed the image of Captain Edgerton. "Heya, Admiral." His hair appeared frazzled.

"Captain Edgerton, we lost contact with you. What's your status? Are you still in the Proxima system?"

"Well, it's been a long journey. Listen, we found your missing pilot, Selene, but we've got bad news." He paused dramatically. "The Krai'kesh took Emma."

"I'm sorry to hear they took Emma, but glad you found Selene. Did you find her in the wreckage?"

"On her home world, Epsilon III, actually. The attack on the system was orchestrated by House Artois. They were doing a 'hostile takeover,' and are working with the Krai'kesh. We've got a boat load of proof thanks to the FIA operatives who were also on the planet."

"I see. So Emma was not taken to Epsilon III?"

"No. Which is why we're contacting you. Do you have any idea where the Krai'kesh fleet may be? Any idea at all?"

Martin shook his head. "Unfortunately not. In fact, they have been hunting..." he stopped, a plan forming in his head. He snapped his fingers. "That's it. The Krai'kesh have been looking for us. They're working with several rogue elements within the Federation. What if we let slip where we are?"

"Then the Krai'kesh will come to you. Dude, that's brilliant."

Martin suppressed irritation at being called dude and smiled. "How soon will you be here? Are you still on the other side of the Federation?"

"We're at Crossroad Station but we've got Isabelle Thorpe with us. We'll make good speed."

"I will leak the information right away, but the enemy might appear before you arrive."

"Just do what you can." The link closed.

Martin turned to Zigana. "Open a channel to Fleet Command. I need to speak to Admiral Hensen."

Admiral Hensen's assistant did not stop them this time and moments later Admiral Hensen appeared on the screen. "Admiral Rigsby. This is a surprise." He made no mention of the attempted attack on Deltar II.

Martin nodded to Admiral Hensen, though it sickened him to do so. "Admiral Hensen. I lied to you before. We are actually located at Pompero IV."

"Ah. Do you require reinforcements?"

"Yes, if you could send aid that would be appreciated." *More like send traitors. I hope we aren't biting off more than we can chew.*

"Of course, Martin. I will dispatch the closest available fleet to your location."

"Thank you, sir."

"One more thing," Admiral Hensen said. "The Joint Chiefs have met. We have appointed Admiral Bordekov as the interim Supreme Commander. Just until we can confirm whether Dawyn Darklance is alive or dead. You understand."

Martin clenched his fists. *Just go along with it. Don't start a fight.* "Yes, sir, I am sure she will fulfill the duties of her office with diligence. I must see to the repairs of the fleet, sir. If you'll excuse me."

"Of course. You will have relief soon." The link closed.

Martin sat back in his chair and let out a huge sigh. "That was one of the hardest things I've ever had to do."

"I believe you convinced him, sir."

"We will see. I hope I didn't make a mistake." He decided to change the subject. "What *is* the status of the repairs? And the re-supply effort."

"Repairs are ninety percent complete across the fleet, sir. Also, the last shipment of munitions just came up from the planet. A fresh batch of pilots, three dozen, arrived along with a dozen new fighters. Each pilot will have a fighter and we have a dozen as backup."

"Good. We'll be ready to face the bastards. As ready as we can be," he amended. "I'll be in my quarters if you need me."

"Very good, sir."

Martin left the bridge and made his way to his quarters.

His wife was taking a nap but awoke when he entered. "Martin, what is it, what's wrong?"

Martin smiled. "Nothing, my dear." He came to sit on the side of the bed by her. She had lost the planet she was governor of to the Krai'kesh. He didn't want to burden her with news they were drawing the Krai'kesh to them intentionally. "How are you?"

"Busy but tired, as you can see. The refugees from my world are scattered and I'm negotiating, though it sounds more like begging, for them to be accepted by other worlds. Unfortunately there are still too many without homes."

"Is there anything I can do?" Martin did not have many contacts in the political scene, but perhaps he could enlist help from other fleets or friends in the military.

His wife shook her head. "No, that's okay dear. This is my cross to bear. I am responsible for those people. Are you going to rest for a while, dear?"

Martin walked around to the other side of the bed and laid down. "Yes, I'm going to lay down for a bit." *While we wait for the boot to drop.*

A BEEP FROM THE COMMUNICATOR woke Martin. He checked the time. Four hours. *That was fast.* He answered the communicator. "Yes?" He already knew what Zigana would say.

"Sir, several void portals are opening," Zigana reported. Proximity alarms blared in the background.

"Signatures," Martin asked as he rose from bed and exited his quarters.

"Several dozen fleets have just arrived."

The ships Dawyn ordered to our sector.

"Perfect timing. Order them to rendezvous with us."

"There's something else, sir. I'm detecting a second set of void portals. These ships have Krai'kesh and Federation architecture, sir."

Martin arrived on the bridge and turned his communicator off.

"Zigana, put me through to Admiral Bellanca," he ordered as he sat down.

"Of course, sir." The display changed to the face of Admiral Bellanca.

"I see the Krai'kesh contacts, Martin. I'm ordering my fleet to join with yours. How did they find us?"

"Thank you, Grace." He hesitated. Would she be angry at his revelation? "I told the usurpers where we were to draw them into a trap. My fleet is going to fall back closer to the planet. Meet us halfway so that we can better support the planet."

"A trap?" Grace asked, pursing her lips. "And you didn't inform me? This is *my* system you're putting at risk, Martin."

"I know, and I am sorry. But we needed the Krai'kesh to arrive because they have Emma Edgerton held captive. Her parents are on their way to attempt a rescue. We have to survive long enough for them to do so."

Grace bowed her head. "Whatever you think is best." The link closed.

Martin sighed. Her anger was an issue for another day. A day when they were not under attack and their survival was in question. "Sound general quarters. Raise shields and bring us to the halfway mark. Use a curving path so our backs are not to the enemy. Launch fighters but keep them close as a screen. How soon before the enemy ships are in range?"

"They are five minutes from missile range, sir, ten from railgun. The time will be different as we're moving away from them. They are launching fighters, however."

"As expected. Tell the CAG to keep our fighters close, even when they engage. Keep them within range of our coilgun batteries so we can support them."

"Yes, sir."

The *Independence* jerked as it turned and began an arcing maneuver that would bring it to the midpoint. The remainder of the fleet followed. Fighters streamed from the carrier and other vessels. He stood and tapped his feet. It wasn't that he wanted to engage the enemy, but the slow maneuvering took its toll on his patience, even after the years of service aboard the carrier. *Let's hope this isn't our* last *journey, old girl.*

"Is the gravity ship with the Krai'kesh forces?"

"No, sir, not yet."

"Let me know as soon as it appears." That thing could bring the entire fleet to ruin.

"There is a larger-than-normal ship among them, sir. It is not emitting a gravity signature like the other ship and does not have the same shape. Plus, we have not seen it before."

"That could be where Emma is being held," Martin mused. There was no way to know for sure.

The proximity alarm sounded again. "What is it this time?"

"A void signature. It's the *Dauntless*, sir."

A void signature. He hadn't heard that term in ten years. Only two individuals in the galaxy could enter or leave shadow space without a portal. "They made good time."

"They're hailing us."

"Put them through."

Moments later Captain Edgerton's face again filled the display. It had only been a few hours but seemed like minutes had passed. "Heya, Admiral. We're here."

Martin shook his head. "The travel speed of Isabelle and her mother are legendary, but I did not know she was *that* fast."

A woman laughed in the background. "My mother is even faster. We travel as fast as thought."

"We are glad for your presence, m'lady. John, we detected a large ship we haven't seen before. Emma could be..."

"She's on there. Ethan can feel her presence."

"Feel her presence?" Martin asked, frowning.

"It's a twin thing," he said, but offered no additional details.

"Well, if you're certain, I suggest waiting until their fleet is engaged with us to strike. Otherwise you will be overwhelmed by their defenses."

John pursed his lips. "I guess you're right," he said after a few moments. "What's it hurt to wait a little longer?"

"My thought exactly."

"On our way to rendezvous with the fleet." The link closed and the icon representing their ship moved toward the *Independence*.

"Sir, enemy fighters are within coilgun range."

The sensor display shifted to show the cluster of fighters closing on the fleet. "Give those fighters everything we have, Zigana."

"Yes, sir."

Martin watched the sensor display as streaks representing streams of bullets and missiles closed on the cloud of enemies. Several enemy icons winked out of existence. The remaining icons continued their path and were soon intermingled with the rest of the Federation fleet. Outside the bridge viewport light flashed and fighters, both Krai'kesh and Federation, flew past. *Brother fighting brother*, Martin thought. *Why did it have to come to this? Why would they betray their own government?* Granted, rebellions had occurred throughout the history of the Federation, and Martin imagined each time someone somewhere wondered the same thing. Did they believe they were "saving" the Federation, were they just following orders out of ignorance or a sense of duty? Martin didn't know, but he could not afford to grant them mercy unless they surrendered. If they wanted a civil war he would give it to them.

"Sir, the first enemy ships are in range of our railguns."

"Federation ships or Krai'kesh?"

"Federation corvettes and frigates."

Why had he asked? It didn't matter. "Target the Federation capital ships. Launch missiles and fire all railgun batteries. Order the rest of the fleet to open fire once they are in range." The more enemies they destroyed or disabled before they reached optimal firing range the better. It was like defending a narrow mountain pass - you had to stop attackers piecemeal if you wanted any chance of surviving.

Zigana fell silent, issuing orders through his implant. A faint vibration rippled up through Martin's legs from railgun recoil. He pictured himself on the wooden or metal ships of old, sailing the seas and engaging in broadside cannon fire exchanges with enemy ships. What would it have been like? Sure, old holos tried to recreate the feeling, but was that authentic?

"One enemy ship destroyed, sir."

Martin refrained from asking the name of the destroyed ship. Perhaps that would ease the pain.

"Continue firing at will," he said. Soon the bigger enemy ships would come into range and then the real fight would begin.

Chapter 17 - Darkness Within

"The *Independence* has engaged the enemy fleet," Derek said aloud.

The *Dauntless* turned sharply and laser fire flashed through where they had been. The top and bottom quad-linked turrets thudded. Two targets disappeared.

"Time to get aboard that big vessel, then," John said. He turned the ship, more smoothly this time, and pointed them toward the oncoming fleet. "Ethan, can you tell *where* in the ship she is?"

"Not until we get closer. Maybe not even then. She feels...different. She isn't responding."

"Can't Isabelle just shift us aboard? Or better yet, go aboard the Krai'kesh ship and bring Emma back?" Derek asked.

"No," Isabelle said.

Derek jerked in surprise. He turned to find her standing in the doorway.

"She does that sometimes," John said. "She's like a damn cat, sneaking around."

Isabelle sniffed. "I love you too, Uncle. But to answer your question, Derek, the void shields around those ships acts like a nullification field, only with concentrated gravity instead of negative energy. I can't shift in or out, but can probably shift inside the ship once we've breached the hull."

"So are we just going to blow a hole in the hull?" Ethan asked.

"I haven't though that far ahead," John said. "Sounds good to me, though."

"Unless it's a chamber Emma is being held in."

"Well, I don't think they have airlocks."

"But their fighters must launch from somewhere, right?"

John snapped his fingers. "Smart kid. Derek, can you locate an opening for us?"

"On it," Derek said, turning back to the sensor console. He narrowed in on the enemy vessel, trying for several minutes to find an entry point. A fighter shot out. He traced it back. "Found it. Below the ship."

"All righty then," John said. "Let's do this." The *Dauntless* neared the enemy cruiser. A railgun shell flashed past. "Geeze, could they have cut it any closer?" He opened a channel to the *Independence*. "Hey, Admiral, could you *not* fire on this big ship until we're aboard? You almost hit us!"

"I figured a skilled pilot like yourself could handle flying in a warzone," the admiral said dryly.

Ashley and Isabelle burst out laughing.

John shot Ashley a glare, his face red.

"What? You're not used to being made fun of in return?" Ashley said.

"If there's nothing else, Captain, I have a battle to fight."

John closed the link without saying anything. "Dick."

Ashley punched him in the shoulder. "Oh, lighten up. You're still one of the best pilots in the galaxy."

"Let's go gear up," Ethan said to Derek.

Isabelle moved out of the way to let them pass, then followed them to the back of the *Dauntless* where the Marines, Selene, and FIA operatives were strapped in. "We're going to be landing inside the Krai'kesh ship soon," Ethan explained. "Unstrap and gear up. We're in for the fight of our lives."

The Marines nodded, unstrapped, and began checking their weapons. Kimberly, Baillidh, and Corbin rose without acknowledging Ethan's words and geared up. "Oi canna wait ta crush some Krai'kesh skulls," Corbin said.

Selene walked up to Derek, wrapped her arms around him, and laid her head on his chest.

Derek patted her on the back, feeling awkward. Yes, they might be about to die but it wasn't really the time for hugging.

"My father was going to kill me," Selene said.

Derek pushed her back to arm's length and looked into her eyes. That was...terrible. "I'm sorry, Selene."

Selene sniffed and wiped a tear from one eye. "All these years I knew he was upset with me but in the back of my mind he was still my father and I kept believing he loved me, deep down. But no, if I hadn't been rescued I was going to be executed tomorrow."

"Selene. There's more to family than just blood." He looked back toward the cockpit. "I've learned that over the years. Sometimes friends and comrades can become closer than family."

Selene nodded. "I've felt that with pilots in the past and most recently with Emma. But even she was taken from me. Why does everyone I get close to get taken away?"

"I'm still here," Derek said.

"For now. You could die during this assault. Hell, *I* could die during this assault. How can I have confidence in any relationship now?"

"By not letting fear of loss paralyze you. It's the people in our lives we care about who give us a reason to live, Selene. Yes, you could push everyone away, but then it would be as if those people had died and you would be lonelier than if you made memories with them."

"I suppose you're right." She kissed him and turned. "Let's gear up."

Derek donned his suit and tested his helmet. He checked the mechanism on his coilgun rifle and that his sidearm, grenades, vibroblade, and other accessories on his utility belt were present.

Isabelle did not carry a rifle, or any weapon. A pair of vibroblades hung from her belt but no guns. "Isabelle, you don't use modern weapons?"

She laughed. "I use them, but I'm not burdened by them on my body." She stretched her arms to the side and two pistols formed from shadowy mist. She twirled them both around and then they disappeared. A rifle appeared in her hand next and she hefted it up and pointed it at the ceiling. A moment later it disappeared. "Any other questions?"

Amazing. "No."

"Hang on, everyone," Ashley said over the intercom. "We're entering the ship." Derek felt a rising sensation.

The two Marines in the quad turrets climbed down and hurried to gear up, while everyone else fell into line behind Ethan, Isabelle, and Derek. John and Ashley came out but wore no armor. "One second," John said. "There probably won't be atmosphere out there until we breach an inner door or something." He went over to an equipment locker and withdrew two disks. He threw one to Ashley. She slapped it on her chest and her armor flowed over her body and solidified. John did the same.

"I want to leave Baillidh behind," Kimberly said. "There's no technology here for him to interface with, so he serves no purpose and would be better off here at the ship in case we need him to fire it up or something."

"Fine with me," John said. He pointed a finger at Baillidh. "Just don't sit in my chair. Got it, B?"

Baillidh nodded. "I will respect your property."

"Smart man. Let's do this," John said. He activated the ramp controls and the ramp descended.

Atmosphere sensors indicated no oxygen beyond the ship. There was gravity, though. The group descended the ramp but found no enemies waiting. "Where are they?" Derek asked through the squad channel.

"Probably waiting to ambush us in tunnels or if we separate," Ethan said. "That's what I would do. If they'd been waiting out here we could have blown them away with our turrets."

"True." Derek searched the wall for signs of a door or controls. All he saw was a bumpy, organic surface with no signs of a doorway.

"So we gonna blow a hole in the wall or something? I don't see a door," John said.

Ashley went up to the wall and put her gloved hand on it.

"Don't touch it!" John scolded her.

She turned and gave him a glare. "I'm a big girl, I can take care of my...ahh," she shrieked and leapt back as the wall melted away to reveal a circular opening. It stayed like that for several moments before coalescing back into a wall.

"So is the entire wall one big door? Or did Ashley just get lucky?" John asked.

"I don't know. But let's just use that," Ethan said. He poked his rifle through, as if waiting to see if it would close on it. It remained open. The others followed. They found themselves in a corridor with walls of the same material as the wall they'd just passed through.

"Which way?" John asked.

"It seems to curve around. So maybe both halls lead to the same place," Ethan speculated.

"Right," John said. He walked to the right. "This is eerie," he said a little while later. "I keep expecting a surge of Krai'kesh to come at us."

"You *want* them to attack us?" Ashley asked.

"Well, no, but I feel like I'm in a haunted house in a horror movie. You know, where they're ignorant and just go in and, like, the suspenseful music plays and they get picked off one-by-one?"

Derek felt goosebumps on his arm. The enemy ship *was* quiet - almost too quiet. No machinery hummed in the distance or reverberated through the floor. Strange organic pods which gave off soft light differed from the harsh lights of Federation ships. Silhouettes of circular doors lined the hall but did not open.

The hall stretched on for what felt like forever. *I think we walked the length of the ship.* At last it opened into a large circular chamber.

A throne sat at the far end of the chamber. A figure sat on the throne, and another stood beside it. The creature on the throne tapped on the arm of it with long finger nails. As the group neared Derek noticed four tentacle-like appendages waving from the rear of the creature's head. It held a staff in its other hand. There did not appear to be any other enemies in the room. "Ah, the heroes of the Federation come at last," the creature boomed.

"Who is this guy?" John asked in the squad channel. "The big kahuna?"

"I'm more concerned with where his guards are. I feel an ambush coming," Ethan said.

"I've seen him before," Selene said. "His name was Overseer Harkesh. He's the one who took..." Selene gasped. "Emma."

Derek looked closer at the figure standing next to the throne. They wore an organic armor but were shorter than the Krai'kesh commanders. They wore no helmet but had hair. Could it be? "Is that Emma?" Derek asked. Her eyes were closed.

"Emma!" Ashley shouted out loud. She took two steps before Ethan grabbed her arm. *Wait, Mother,* Ethan said through their shared channel.

"Here we are," John said aloud. "You could have just called us up, you know. You didn't have to abduct our daughter to get to talk to us."

The overseer laughed and stood. He stood taller than the commanders Derek had seen before. "I did not take your daughter just to talk with you. Just as you do not speak to the ants beneath your feet. No, I took your daughter to bring about your demise. She will be your end." He stretched a hand to his right.

Emma opened her eyes. Dark green orbs glared at the group.

Ashley took a step back. "No," she said aloud. "No, Emma, no."

"You can fight this," Selene said. "You told me you would fight."

"She cannot hear you, any more than the dog can hear the flea," Overseer Harkesh said. "But do not worry. Soon you will be dead and have no cares. Your deaths will please the god-emperor."

"Are you this 'god-emperor,' then?" John asked. He must have been fishing for information, since Selene had said his title.

"I am but a humble servant of Rae'Shela. As is your daughter, now. Go, my pet, destroy these intruders."

Emma extended her right arm and a blade of coral-like material grew out from her gauntlet. She lifted her left and a tentacle extended from that gauntlet. She advanced in silence, green eyes glowing and teeth gritted.

A roar came from behind. Derek spun and found a swarm of over a dozen Krai'kesh skitterers being herded toward them by commanders. "Behind us!" Derek warned.

"Do not hurt Emma," Ethan said. "Leave her to me."

"I'll help too," Derek said.

"As will I," Selene said.

"Ashley and I will get this overseer guy," John said. "Everyone else, focus on the Krai'kesh."

The remainder of the Marines, as well as Kimberly, Corbin, and Isabelle, turned to face the newcomers. Two pistols materialized in Isabelle's hands and she fired coilgun shells at the oncoming horde.

Derek ran up to Ethan. *What's the plan?* he asked in a direct communication to Ethan and Selene.

I'm still working that out, Ethan admitted. *I don't know what they did to her. I just hope she doesn't have her magic.*

As if she knew what her brother had said, Emma threw a fireball at the trio.

Ethan deflected it into the floor with ease. *That answers that question. Spread out and keep her distracted. I don't want her harmed!*

How are you going to incapacitate her if you don't harm her? Derek thought. *I think he might be too close to the situation.*

Off to the side, Ashley threw a fireball at the overseer. It came close but then hit an invisible barrier and dissolved.

Damn it! Ashley said to the whole squad channel. *He's got a nullification field.*

Yeah, see that crystal on his belt? It's the Fields of Pelinor all over again, John said.

Except no Dawyn here to stick a sword in it.

We'll just have to improvise. Ashley drew a pistol and started firing at the overseer, but her bullets were absorbed into a singularity like with ordinary commanders.

Derek leapt back as Emma lashed out with her whip. She pursued him, tentacle flailing around. Selene tried to shoot her with a laser, set to stun, but Emma's armor absorbed it and she exhibited no signs of being inhibited. When she swung again Derek raised his rifle and the tentacle wrapped around it. He felt a moment of victory before the tentacle crushed the rifle, breaking it in two. *Imagine if that were my neck*, he thought. She followed up by darting forward with the blade stretching from her right gauntlet. Derek raised his arms to block and braced for impact.

Ethan blocked Emma's follow-up strike with his vibroswords right before they struck home. He stepped in front of Derek and pushed back. But the suit Emma wore gave her more strength than Derek expected a woman of her stature to have and Ethan was forced to take a step back. "Don't...do...this...Emma," he grunted.

Emma did not respond other than to growl and bring her whip swinging around toward his neck.

Derek stepped forward on instinct. He put his arm out and the whip wrapped around his arm. For a moment, nothing happened. Then pain came. Horrendous pain. He heard screaming and it took him a moment to realize it was himself screaming. He heard bone crunching, felt it shattering beneath his skin even through armor.

He vaguely noticed Selene rushing forward. She tackled Emma and sent her hurtling to the floor. Derek flopped down, pulled by the tentacle before it released his arm and coiled to strike at Selene.

Ethan swung both blades and they clanged as they met in the center, slicing the tentacle in half. It was Emma's turn to scream. Was she connected to the armor somehow? Did she feel the tentacle being severed in some way? Such thoughts faded as his vision blurred from the pain. He pleaded with the universe to bring unconsciousness but it did not come. Instead he watched as Ethan kicked Emma in the head with a boot. She fell silent.

Selene stepped back. "What happened to not harming her?" she asked aloud.

"There's a line between not harming someone and letting them harm others." He pointed at Derek.

Derek groaned in response. He felt his adrenaline fading and darkness took him.

KIMBERLY TURNED FROM where her old friend lay unconscious on the floor and aimed at a skitterer which was harassing two Marines. She couldn't get a clear shot. *Get the hell out of the way*, she thought. She didn't want to shoot an ally in the back. They were short enough on allies as it was. Her opportunity came when one of the Marines fell backward, shoved by a Krai'kesh claw. Not looking to see if the Marine was injured, Kimberly fired at the skitterer's center mass. It paused in its follow-up strike and looked at her. *Well, that made it mad*, she thought. She fired again, buying time for the fallen Marine to scuttle backward out of reach of their attacker's claws and pincers.

The creature didn't care about the Marine any longer, however, for it skittered toward Kimberly now. She continued to fire and was joined by the Marine she'd saved and Corbin. "Why do ye always make yer enemies mad?" he asked.

Kimberly shrugged. "It's a gift, I guess." *A curse is more like it.*

"Well tis a good thing oi'm here den, eh?"

"If you save me, you'll be my hero," Kimberly said. "But right now," she grunted as she fired faster, depressing and releasing the trigger as fast as she could, "that's in question."

"Bah! Take dis ye bastard!" He withdrew a grenade, removed the pin, held it for two seconds and tossed it toward the oncoming assailant. It exploded, sending the skitterer flying backward. It did not get up. "Do oi get a kiss from da damsel in distress?" he asked, puckering up.

Kimberly raised one eyebrow. "There are at least a dozen more left before I give you a kiss. Get to it."

Corbin bowed. "Right away, yer highness."

She rolled her eyes. "Before it was m'lady, now it's your highness. What next, 'your majesty?'"

"Ye'll always be the queen of me heart," Corbin said.

"Here come some more dragons, knight in shining armor." She pointed to where two commanders were shoving aside skitterers to get to the front.

"'Tis all worth it fer a kiss," Corbin said, turning and firing at a nearby enemy.

Buffs of shadowy mist marked Isabelle's movements as she moved from enemy to enemy, using blade and bullet or laser to strike at the Krai'kesh. She appeared behind one of the newcomer commanders and stabbed at their back. They grunted in pain and swept their bladed staff out behind them but struck only dark mist and air. She appeared above her target and fired two bullets toward their helmet before disappearing again.

That must become tiring, Kimberly thought. *But she's faced worse.* She remembered when Isabelle had fought a massive mutant during the viral outbreak on Galatia IV. She had been hiding behind a console, clutching her father's datapad to her chest, while she created a veritable ring of shadow around the monster. It was that day, despite everything else that had happened, that she decided she wanted to be an FIA agent.

She took aim at another skitterer.

SELENE KNELT AT DEREK's side. His helmet had deactivated and she felt for a pulse. He was breathing, but it was shallow. *We have to get out of here,* she said over the squad channel. *Derek is hurt and Emma is unconscious.*

Ethan knelt beside Emma, though he did not check for a pulse. Her chest was rising and falling. Instead he ran his hands over the armor she wore. Perhaps looking for a seam.

John and Ashley faced the overseer and seemed to have met their match. Every flame Ashley threw at the towering enemy absorbed into his armor. He swept his staff from side-to-side, forcing John and Ashley back. John fought back with his sword and kept it at bay.

"You are no match for me, pitiful humans," the overseer taunted. "You, Lord of Light, where is your precious sunlight now?"

"I don't need sunlight to kick your ass," John replied.

Something his father said affected Ethan, for he rose and spoke in the squadron channel. *All forces, turn and fire your laser weapons at my father on my mark. Get ready, Dad.*

Toss some flash-bangs in there while you're at it, son, John said.

Fire on John? But why? She thought. Yet she trained her weapon on him.

All the Marines had turned. Only Isabelle had not, for she was too busy darting around to create a screen while they were pre-occupied.

Fire! Ethan ordered. He tossed four flash-bangs toward John's feet and then suited action to words and fired at his father.

The lasers converged on John's back, but instead of burning him they hit an invisible barrier. The barrier began to glow white. He lifted his sword and the light flowed into him, up his arms, and into his sword. It glowed yellow.

Keep firing! Ethan said.

I can't hold them much longer, Isabelle said. *Hurry up.*

The sword changed from yellow to red as more laser energy slammed into his shield. The flash-bangs exploded. Red became orange and transformed into white. *I'm ready,* John said.

The Marines and FIA operatives turned their attention back to the Krai'kesh, but Selene's eyes were riveted on the glowing sword that burned bright like the sun. The light seared her eyes, causing her implant to dim her visor.

John stepped forward, his footsteps leaving burn marks in the organic floor. He lowered the sword and pointed it at the overseer.

Overseer Harkesh took a step back. "Impossible," he said.

"Send your god-emperor our regards when you get to hell," John said. "And tell him he's next."

"You may kill me, but I will go on to glory at the right hand of Rae."

"Just keep telling yourself that," John said. He hefted the sword again and brought the hilt up next to his head. He roared and charged the overseer.

The overseer tried to block the blade, but the point where staff met blade melted and the staff broke in two.

The blade continued its path. John roared. "For Emma!" and sliced the overseer in half diagonally.

A shocked expression appeared on the overseer's face before the two halves of him fell to the floor. A small amount of blood pooled on the floor beneath him, though the blade had cauterized the wound.

John turned. *Everyone down!* he shouted through the link. *Get on the ground!*

Everyone, except Isabelle, dropped to their stomachs. Selene positioned herself so she could see John.

Isabelle continued fighting a commander in melee combat. *Just do it,* she said through the link.

John nodded and leveled his sword at the remaining Krai'kesh.

Two skitterers attempted to take advantage of the perceived weakness of their opponents and charged forward.

A beam of light burst out from the sword, flowing straight toward the charging skitterers. They evaporated like water hitting a hot stove, turning to ash in a second. The beam expanded to the left and right. It burnt through every enemy it touched, commanders and skitterers alike. *Move, Isabelle,* John said.

Isabelle disappeared into the shadow realm a moment before the beam passed through where she had been, overwhelmed the shield of the overseer and burnt them to a crisp.

Selene let out a deep sigh. They'd done it!

"Let's get out of here," John said. "Can two Marines carry Derek?"

Ethan bent down and picked his sister up.

The group made their way out of the audience chamber, two other Marine corpses being carried and one Marine limping from a wound in his leg, back down the hall they'd come down and to the *Dauntless.* It appeared unmolested. The ramp lowered and John limped aboard first.

John and Ashley went up to the cockpit while Ethan carried Selene to med bay and two other Marines followed with Derek. Selene decided to follow John and Ashley. She couldn't bear to see Derek in that state.

"...*Independence*, this is the *Dauntless*. I say again, we have rescued Emma and killed the overseer. We are returning."

"Acknowledged...*Dauntless*...interfer...void..."

"Something is causing interference," John pointed out. "But what?" He flew the *Dauntless* out of the belly of the Krai'kesh ship. "Oh, shit," he said.

There, emerging from a massive void portal, was the gravity ship the fleet had encountered before.

"We're all gonna die," he said.

"Can oi get that kiss now?" Selene heard Corbin ask. "Before we get destroyed?"

"No," Kimberly said.

Selene couldn't help but smile, though it disappeared as she thought of Derek lying unconscious in the back.

Chapter 18 - Black Hole

"Sir, the gravity ship has emerged."

"I see it," Martin said, studying the sensor display. It had emerged behind the enemy lines. For a moment it did not move. What was it waiting for? "Continue firing on the rest of the Krai'kesh and rogue Federation fleet. Our weapons can't hurt that ship, we already saw that. Might as well focus on what we *can* kill. *And hope for a miracle*, he thought.

"The *Dauntless* is returning to us. Their communication was garbled but it appears they killed an overseer of some sort."

"They must have rescued Emma or they would not be returning," Martin surmised. He pushed the Eternal family out of his mind for a moment. "What is the status of our defenses?"

"Several gun batteries have been destroyed, our fighters are down to a dozen and our shield capacity is at forty percent. There are fires on decks seven, sixteen, and twenty-two. Crews are working to contain them."

Martin sighed. "Is the rest of the fleet faring so well?"

"All ships loyal to us are taking heavy damage, sir. Admiral Bellanca's ships and the reinforcing fleets included. Several dozen ships have been destroyed. Would you like me to list them?"

Martin waved. "No. We don't have time for that and it doesn't matter at this point." There would be time to mourn the dead and remember them later. Right now they were fighting for their lives. "To fight or retreat," he whispered.

"Pardon me, sir?"

"I'm trying to decide whether to continue fighting or retreat." If they retreated, Pompero IV would be lost. Millions of civilians still on the planet would be killed as surely as the sun in the east each morning on Tar Ebon. But if they didn't retreat they would be destroyed and Pompero IV and countless other worlds would fall. He thought of the oath he had taken upon enlisting and re-affirmed upon being granted command of the *Independence*. To carry out the duties of the Federation faithfully until death or until his service was fulfilled. There were many who had broken that oath, rogue elements, but there were many more who had died, today and in the days and weeks prior. He could not dishonor their sacrifice again. "We fight," he said. "We fight until our last breath and then we keep on fighting." The more enemy ships they destroyed the less the rest of the Federation fleets would need to fight later on.

The gravity ship started moving. It passed through the enemy lines and made its way toward the *Independence*. It moved fast for such a huge ship. Perhaps the gravity wells it generated helped propel it? Martin didn't know for sure. He wasn't a scientist by any stretch. All he knew was the end was staring him in the proverbial face. He thought of his wife and children. He considered bringing them up on the bridge and giving them one final embrace. Or sending them into an escape pod, kicking and screaming if necessary, and shooting it toward Pompero IV. No. His wife would never forgive him for that.

"How long before the gravity ship is in range?" Martin asked.

"Three minutes, sir. Shall we direct fire at it?"

"No." He resigned himself to their fate and sat down in his chair. "Continue firing on the other ships."

"As you say, sir."

Time seemed to slow as the gravity ship closed the distance. Martin could not take his eyes away from the sensor display. He stood again and walked to the viewport. He could see, out the side of the viewport.

The great destroyer. The *Independence* shook as the gravity ship exerted its power on them. Damage alarms blared, pipes burst, and glass at several consoles shattered. Martin steadied himself on a support beam.

He knew it was futile, but at least his crew might have a chance. They could hide on the planet or escape on a transport. Maybe. "Zigana, order evac..."

"Sir," Zigana interrupted. "I'm detecting a new void signature in front of us."

Another signature. "Isabelle is with the *Dauntless*. That means it must be Bridgette. Why would she bring them out of shadow space right in front of the gravity ship? Do they have a death wish?" He didn't think even the power of their shifting magic was enough to stop the gravity waves emitted by the enemy vessel.

"Its identifier lists it as the *Renegade*, sir. It's a smaller vessel. They're right in the path of the gravity beam."

What they hell are they doing?

RACHEL TURNED AND LOOKED at her aunt. She had not opened the side airlock yet.

"Good luck," Bridgette said. "The galaxy is depending on you. But no pressure." She disappeared into shadow space.

"Don't let her get to you, ma'am," Reynaldo said. "You got this."

"If you don't, we'll all be dead," Maggie said.

"Thank you for pointing out the obvious," Rachel said. "How did I end up with such a loyal crew?"

"You were the winning side," Maggie said, smirking. "Don't disappoint us."

Rachel gave her a mock salute. "I'll do my best." *I don't want to die...again...either.* She closed the blast door separating the atmosphere of the *Renegade* from the depth of space and hit the lever to lower the ramp. Red warning lights blared and seconds later the ramp lowered. Air whooshed past her, pulling her along with it like rip tides pulling a swimmer out to sea. She oriented herself and anchored herself with gravity so she floated motionless in the depth of space.

A massive ship floated in front of her. She felt waves of gravity emanating out of it and pummeling the star carrier behind her. Waves slammed into the *Renegade* too, bucking it like a buoy caught in high waves. *Hang on*, she thought. She turned back to the enemy ship. *This ends, now*, she thought, unable to speak in the void of space. She closed her eyes and drew fully upon her power. She no longer felt her body, only gravity. She felt the pull of the sun, strong despite the distance. She felt the smaller pull of the nearby planet and its moon. She felt the pull of distant planets in the solar system and nearby stars. All the gravity waves emitted by every celestial body within dozens of light years pummeled her consciousness. Compared to such waves the ship in front of her was nothing but a pebble dropped in the ocean. She focused on the enemy ship. She felt its gravity shield, felt a foreign mechanism drawing the natural gravity waves found all around it into itself. She likened it to a pump sucking water up from a pool. It was time to drain the pool.

She cast out her hands and imagined a barrier around the enemy ship. A barrier which blocked gravity that would not permit it to reach the gravity pump. It worked. She saw in her mind's eye the waves bouncing off her barrier, sliding around the bubble she'd created. The enemy's gravity shield faltered, the waves it had been flinging toward the Federation ship and the *Renegade* stopped. *Now*, she thought, this time directing it into her implant, which, through the *Renegade's* communication array, was sent to her intended audience.

MARTIN STARED SLACK-jawed as the hazy swirling darkness around the gravity ship disappeared. The gravity waves had stopped too. "How?" was the only word he could muster.

"Sir, we're detecting yet another void signature. Above the gravity ship."

Martin did not look at Zigana, his eyes transfixed on the sight before him.

There, materializing not piecemeal like a ship traveling through a void portal, but all at once, was the largest ship Martin had ever seen. "My God," he said.

A ping indicated an incoming communication. "Video communication coming in, sir."

Martin stepped back to in front of his chair so he could see the communication. The communication display morphed into the image of Dawyn Darklance. Martin gasped.

"This is Supreme Commander Dawyn Darklance of the Federation Navy. I am speaking to all loyal Federation forces. Today is our day. The dawn has come. Let us banish the darkness once and for all."

Several crew members let out cheers. Martin, despite feeling shock, found himself wearing a wide grin.

Dawyn's expression became angry. "And to the Krai'kesh and their human allies. Know this. Your days are numbered. You chose your side and now we will send you to meet your god-emperor. May he have mercy on your soul, for you will find none from me. Now witness the fury of the *Nightblade*."

Indeed, the sensor display identified the new ship as the *Nightblade* mark II. Moments later the screen filled with lights, colors, and icons as the ship attacked. Martin went back to the viewport to watch.

Railguns, dozens of them, fired streams of shells at the gravity ship and other vessels. Dozens, perhaps hundreds, of missiles erupted from the flank of the ship and streaked off in every direction. Concentrated beams of red laser light shot out from dozens of laser batteries too.

From beneath came hundreds of small objects. "What are those?" Martin wondered aloud.

"They appear to be un-manned drones, sir," Zigana answered.

"Drones?" That was experimental, and restricted, technology. But it was the Supreme Commander they were talking about. And the enemy was the Krai'kesh. It was worth the risk.

The drones moved in packs toward the enemy fleet, ignoring the gravity ship. For its part, the gravity ship looked like it had sustained heavy damage. It had relied on its shield so much it lacked traditional armor. Super-heated chunks of hull flew off into space while railgun shells peppered it like meteorites striking the surface of a moon. A few minutes after the *Nightblade* arrived the gravity ship was shattered, its pieces flying off in every direction and creating a miniature asteroid field.

The *Renegade* took off from where it had been floating stationary in space and headed toward the *Nightblade* where it flew inside.

The remaining Krai'kesh and rogue Federation forces did not stand a chance against the onslaught brought by the *Nightblade*. Not that they didn't try, but their projectiles were destroyed by overlapping fields of coilgun fire and their lasers met an energy shield. Meanwhile they were overwhelmed. One ship tried to surrender, but Dawyn paid their communication no mind and the ship exploded a minute later.

"I will allow survivors in escape pods to be picked up," Dawyn said on the global channel broadcast to all ships, friend and foe. "But no traitorous vessels shall be spared."

Soon the Krai'kesh and rogue vessels tried to retreat. The loyalist ships pursued them. Only a handful of enemy ships managed to escape to shadow space.

Within half an hour of the arrival of the *Renegade* the battle was over. Martin breathed a sigh of relief and slumped in his chair. He put his head in his hands and sobbed. They were not tears of sadness but joy at surviving. *It was a miracle*, he thought.

"Sir, the *Nightblade* is hailing us."

Martin lifted his head, wiped his eyes and cleared his throat. "Put it through."

Dawyn appeared on the display. "Martin, my old friend. I am glad you survived."

"Glad that *I survived*?" Martin asked. "With all due respect, sir, it was *you* who was presumed dead."

"I assure you, the duplicity was necessary. While I did not intend for the original *Nightblade* to be destroyed, I was prepared for such an eventuality."

Martin shook his head. Prepared for a betrayal from within? And where had the massive ship come from? He had so many questions. "I understand, sir," he said.

Dawyn laughed. "I can see you don't. I want you to come over to the *Nightblade*. You can hitch a ride on the *Dauntless*. I'm calling a strategy meeting."

"Of course, sir. I am on my way."

Chapter 19 - Reunited

Martin descended the *Dauntless'* ramp and stared in wonder at the massive docking bay inside the *Nightblade*. *They could fit a hundred fighters in here, easily*, he thought.

Dawyn was not waiting for them but had instructed them to come to the bridge. Markers on the wall led him and the others to a transporter tube which carried them across the length of the ship to the bridge. The bridge impressed Martin even more than the docking bay. Pristine consoles lined the walls, an advanced tactical command station sat vacant near the captain's chair. A tactical display table sat in front of the captain's chair, and that is where Martin found the other guests.

He recognized Bridgette and Dawyn, but one of the guests caused him to stop in his tracks. "President Galantos?" he blurted.

The president turned and smiled. "Ah, Admiral Rigsby, it is good to finally meet you in person!" The president stepped forward and offered his hand.

Martin shook it. The other guests he could picture being there, even the unknown ones, but the president of the Federation? "With respect, sir. How, or better yet, why, are you here?"

"Well, it's a long story, so join us and Dawyn will brief us all on what's happened."

"Nice ship, dude," John said to Dawyn. "You were holding out on us this whole time?"

"I had to keep it a secret," Dawyn said. "From everyone."

"So who helped you build this? Not that you aren't smart...just saying."

"Our mutual brother-in-law."

"*Jason?*" John and Bridgette said in unison.

"Correct." Dawyn smiled and looked at Bridgette. "He was not being a 'deadbeat' husband but was in fact helping to remotely build the vessel we are standing on. I hope that mollifies you a bit."

Bridgette nodded and smirked. "It does explain why he was so consumed by work that he couldn't spent time with me."

"I believe introductions are in order," Dawyn said. He proceeded to introduce his daughter and her companions, the FIA agents and the Eternals. Many already seemed to know one another, for Martin noticed Kimberly staring at Rachel across the table and Rachel in turn glaring at Isabelle, but he did not have time to try to unravel all the connections.

"Now that's out of the way, we need to talk strategy." He beckoned to the tactical display, which morphed into a list of fleets and planets. "The Krai'kesh suffered a major setback here today. Their super weapon was destroyed, as was most of their fleet. However, they are not destroyed."

"Nope, we only killed the overseer of the Krai'kesh," John said. "It sounded like the god-emperor was still out there."

Dawyn nodded. "Correct. And I highly doubt he was aboard the gravity ship Rachel so soundly dealt with. It would have been a stupid move for him to do such a thing."

"So that means the war isn't over?" Ashley asked.

"Not by a long shot. But, we have bigger problems. Isabelle, would you care to explain?"

Isabelle nodded. "My agents," she gestured to her three agents, "discovered a mass infiltration effort by the Krai'kesh. They were aided by certain houses in the Commerce Sector," her gaze flickered to Selene for a moment, "to spread throughout the Federation undetected. We have a partial list of their locations but still do not know the full extent of their spread or how long they have been in our galaxy prior to the invasion. We have to assume they have been gathering intelligence and allies alike during their time here."

John whistled. "Wow, that's a lot to digest. And are those Krai'kesh related to this rebellion that's going on?"

"Yes and no," Bridgette said. "The human traitors are adherents of the 'Cult of Rae,' a group of religious zealots who worship the god-emperor of the Krai'kesh." She raised a hand when John opened his mouth. "Don't ask me why. While these traitors likely would have rebelled on their own, they're the type to latch onto any cause that suits their goals, they were emboldened by Krai'kesh elements in our galaxy which spread the gospel of their god-emperor and radicalized them."

"So it's like the vultures coming to feast on a carcass. All the traitors came flying down when they smelled blood," John said.

"Correct."

"So we have two problems now," Dawyn said. "We have to contend with this rebellion, which has reached as high as Fleet Command and Tar Ebon, hence the presence of the president, who barely escaped with his life. Secondly, we must prepare our defenses for the next wave of Krai'kesh. I have a feeling this incursion was only an exploratory fleet, sent to make way for the full invasion fleet. We must crush this rebellion swiftly and present a united front against the Krai'kesh. If we are divided we will fall."

"Does that include the Empire?" Martin asked.

Dawyn nodded. "Yes, we must bring the Empire into the fold. We cannot continue to keep ships on the Imperium Line. We have to convince them to join the Federation or at the least sign an alliance with us."

"What of the Commerce Sector?" Selene asked.

"They will be given a choice. Ally with us and renounce their ties with the Krai'kesh or be destroyed."

"That is more than they deserve," Selene said.

Dawyn held her gaze for a few extra moments before nodding. Was he surprised at the vehemence in her voice? She was from House Artois after all. Would she be okay with her house being destroyed? "I understand a Marine who worked closely with the Edgerton's and Emma were both wounded in the fight with the overseer?"

Ethan spoke. "Emma was taken over by the overseer somehow. We knocked her unconscious but she appears to be in a coma. We have her under observation until we can have doctors look at her."

"Perhaps Jason can examine her now that his work on this project is done," Dawyn said. "And the Marine?"

John cleared his throat. "He suffered a broken, well, crushed, arm, but is awake and recovering."

"He risked his life to save mine," Ethan said. "He deserves a medal."

"And he will get one. Most of you in this room deserve medals. Although we prepared for this day as best we could, none of us could anticipate what actually came out from the void. We will do our best to survive this and we *will* be prepared to fight the next wave."

Connect with the Author

The author loves to connect with fans. You can reach him through any of these methods:

1. Email him at dayne@darkstarpublishing.com
2. Visit his Facebook page at https://www.facebook.com/ SagaOfTheSevenStars[1]/ and give his page a like.
3. Follow him on Twitter. His handle is @dayne87

Review this book and receive a free copy of the next!

If you review this book and leave a review on your favorite public site and send me a link to it as proof, you will receive a free copy of my second book once it is finished!

Just email proof of your review (a link to where it's posted) to admin@darkstarpublishing.com. Thanks!

Join our mailing list

Join our mailing list by visiting http://eepurl.com/b7th21 and signing up. You will receive a free copy of the first issue of SciFan Magazine for FREE. SciFan Magazine is packed with science fantasy stories from very talented authors.

Don't miss out!

Visit the website below and you can sign up to receive emails whenever Dayne Edmondson publishes a new book. There's no charge and no obligation.

https://books2read.com/r/B-A-ZEND-OINR

BOOKS 2 READ

Connecting independent readers to independent writers.

Did you love *Ruin*? Then you should read *Ghost Ranger* by Dayne Edmondson!

My name is Rachel. I **died and rose again**.

I was an ordinary high school girl when a viral plague spread across my planet. Those that died rose again as mindless zombies. Fortunately, science came to the rescue and gave me back my mind. As a conscious zombie, I gained exceptional powers – speed, strength and more. That, plus a secret heritage, changed my life forever.

The outside world didn't accept my kind, however, and soon I decided to join the military. I trained to become an Army Ranger.

Now, as an elite undead killing machine, I must make a choice. Allegiance to my kind or to the Federation. Choose wrong and I could die...for good.

Another installment in the Seven Stars Universe by Dayne Edmondson, this is a young adult space opera adventure novel set a few years before his space opera novel "Emergence" and featuring a major character from the third book, "Ruin."

Buy now to jump into the adventure.

Read more at https://www.darkstarpublishing.com.

Also by Dayne Edmondson

The Dark Tide Trilogy
Emergence
Eclipse
Ruin

The Mageborn Saga
Mageborn
The Cursed Tower
Halls of Light

The Seven Stars Universe
Ghost Ranger
Space Commando

The Shadow Trilogy
Blood and Shadows
Time of Shadows
Shadows Fall

Standalone
The Complete Dark Tide Trilogy
The Complete Shadow Trilogy

Watch for more at https://www.darkstarpublishing.com.

About the Author

Dayne Edmondson lives in southeastern Michigan with his wife and two young children, a boy and a girl. He writes part time and works a day job.

His books can be read in this order:

The Shadow Trilogy:
1. Blood and Shadows
2. Time of Shadows
3. Shadows Fall

Mageborn Saga:
1. Mageborn
2. The Cursed Tower
3. Halls of Light (coming 2019)

The Seven Stars Universe:
1. Ghost Ranger (coming 2019)

The Dark Tide Trilogy:
1. Emergence
2. Eclipse
3. Ruin

Dayne enjoys reading, writing, the occasional video game, watching TV with his wife, walking and spending time with his children indoors or out.

He writes and reads science fiction and fantasy. Some of his favorite authors/books include Robert Jordan, Brandon Sanderson, (almost) all the Star Wars EU books, Elizabeth Haydon, Christopher Nuttall and more.

Read more at https://www.darkstarpublishing.com.

About the Publisher

Dark Star Publishing is a small-press publisher of science fiction and fantasy novels. They place particular emphasis on books written **in** the Seven Stars Universe (the universe created by author and owner Dayne Edmondson).

For more information, visit https://www.darkstarpublishing.com

www.ingramcontent.com/pod-product-compliance
Lightning Source LLC
Chambersburg PA
CBHW051244250626
47155CB00009B/3156